Camilla Isley is an  engineer who left her job to follow her husband...

She's a cat lover, coffee addict, and shoe hoarder. Besides writing, she loves reading—duh!—cooking, watching bad TV, and going to the movies—popcorn, please. She's a bit of a foodie, nothing too serious.

A keen traveler, Camilla knows mosquitoes play a role in the ecosystem, and she doesn't want to starve all those frog princes out there, but she could really live without them.

You can find out more about her here: **www.camillaisley.com** and by following her on Instagram or Facebook.

@camillaisley
facebook.com/camillaisley

By the Same Author

Opposites ♡ Attract

(An Enemies to Lovers Romantic Comedy)
First Comes Love
Book 1

Camilla Isley

This is a work of fiction. Names, characters, businesses, places, events and incidents either are products of the author's imagination or are used fictitiously. Any resemblance to actual events or locales or persons, living or dead, is entirely coincidental.

Dedication

To all single moms who are looking for love…

One

Lucas

A woman in a red coat rushes in front of me in the subway station, cutting me off at the yellow line marking the end of the platform. Chivalry prevents me from protesting aloud or asserting my right to board the train first and compels me to pause for a second to let her pass.

It's one second too many.

The moment she steps into the subway car, the doors slide shut and the train begins to move, leaving me behind gaping like an idiot at the beautiful profile of the woman in red who stole my ride. I barely have time to take in the regular curve of her nose, heart-shaped mouth, and dark hair swept back in a bun before the train gathers speed and they both disappear into the tunnel ahead.

On the ceiling, the subway monitor informs me another train is due in ten minutes. Fingers crossed it'll be on time; otherwise, I'm going to be late, and I can't afford to be. I've spent months hunting for a new office, ever since the rent on my current space skyrocketed and I had no choice but to cancel the lease. But so far, I've had no luck. All the places I've seen were out of my budget or not to my taste—as in, they wouldn't be to any sane human being's taste, unless they favored dingy holes with no light, no windows, stained walls, and fifty-year-old carpet.

And the clock's ticking—not just to get to my appointment, but to find a new place, too, as I have to move out of my office next week. In short, I have everything staked

1

on the newly-renovated business complex I'm supposed to be visiting in less than an hour, assuming I can make it to Brooklyn Heights in time.

Luckily, the next train pulls into the station on the dot, and, with no other corner-cutters in heels before me, I hop in first and even find an empty seat.

Aha.

Now I can get to my appointment on time, and I don't have to grab onto an overhead handle while being jostled right and left, as that red-wearing woman is surely doing right now.

Despite the unexpected setback, I reach my destination with fifteen minutes to spare; just enough time to grab a quick breakfast first. I find a Starbucks in my path that's surprisingly not too busy, so I step in and give the female barista my standard order.

"Tall cappuccino, double espresso shot, easy on the foam. And a donut, please."

"Right away, sir." The young woman behind the counter smiles at me. "Could I have your name, please?"

"Lucas," I say. "Luke is fine."

Her smile widens. "Luke it is." The barista rings up my order, and frowns. "I'm sorry, sir, it looks like we're out of donuts. Could I get you anything else to eat?"

Disappointed, I take a quick look at the bakery display. "A blueberry muffin is okay, thanks."

I pay and move to the other end of the line to wait for my drink. In my peripheral vision, I catch a flash of red and turn toward it... And why am I not surprised to see a heart-shaped mouth bite down on a mouthwatering, double-glazed donut?

What should've been *my* donut.

Looking away from both woman and pastry, I try to convince myself the muffin is going to taste just as delicious as the donut.

It won't.

When my cappuccino is ready, I move outside, since it's a sunny day none too cold for March in New York. I hate eating and walking, so I sit at one of the metal tables and sniff the muffin.

Mmm.

Halfway through my first bite, the woman in red leaves the coffee shop. She strolls down the street without a care in the world. Her coat flaps open as she walks, revealing a black skirt suit underneath. The skirt is so tight it forces her to take small steps, while her black stiletto heels make a click-clack sound as they hit the concrete.

That queue-jumping, donut-stealing witch. I hope I'll never see her again.

I finish my breakfast and check my watch. Time to go.

The address Leslie—my new real estate agent, and the girlfriend of my best friend, Garrett—gave me brings me to one of those industrial rehabilitations. Before the area was gentrified, the complex must've been a factory now turned into lofts and offices. I take to the place at once, liking that history dwells within these walls and that the building isn't a brand-new high-rise with no soul.

In the entry hall, I check in at the reception and they direct me to take the elevator to the third floor. The elevator is another surprise. Whoever remodeled this lot has an impeccable sense of style and kept the old freight machine instead of opting for a new, shiny metal box that would've clashed with the retro, historical vibe of the structure. The interior has been refurbished to transport people with a polished casing, while the metal frame has a distressed paint effect easily recognizable as a design choice rather than spontaneous wear and tear. Admittedly, the journey to the top is on the slower side, but, hey, one can't have everything.

Once the elevator stops, I step out on the small landing facing three doors. On my left, a double set of industrial metal and glass doors is half-open. Behind its panes, white desks equipped with monitors fill the space. The office seems already running and busy. A bronze plate informs me these are the headquarters of Inceptor Magazine. Never heard of it. Must be some kind of hip startup, judging from how young and trendy its working force looks.

In front of me, there's a closed wooden door—less glamorous than the glass one but more practical, perhaps. And, on the left, Leslie is coming out of a similar, regular wooden door.

"Lucas." Her bright smile falters as she spots me, and my heart sinks with a surefire realization: *I'm too late.* "I'm so sorry," she says. "But I've just rented out the office I wanted to show you."

My shoulders sag, and because I must be a masochist, I glance beyond the wide-open door to get a peek at the space I'm sure would've been perfect.

Instead, I catch sight of a woman in a red coat bent over the single piece of furniture in the room—a white desk—as she signs the lease to my dream office.

Oh, hell no!

I barge in. "Not you again," I say.

The woman jolts and straightens up. She turns to me, holding the papers in one hand and the pen in the other.

Big brown eyes set on me with a glint of curiosity. "I'm sorry," she says. "Do we know each other?"

"No, but you cut in front of me on the subway this morning, making me miss the train. Then you ate the last donut at Starbucks. And now you're stealing my dream office."

The woman in red doesn't so much as blink. "I've no idea what you're talking about. But I know that as of a minute ago, I'm officially leasing this space, which means you're trespassing on private property." She calmly replaces the cap to the pen and drops it on the table, brandishing her papers at me. "So, I suggest you show yourself out before I call the police."

My mouth gapes open. It takes all my self-control not to utter any of the many rude retorts streaming through my mind.

The woman walks up to me and stops, adding, "If I could make a suggestion, though, screaming at strangers isn't a super healthy way to cope with your frustrations. Maybe you should see a therapist about anger management."

I glare at her. "I *am* a therapist!"

"Really?" She scoffs. "I presume you don't help people deal with self-control, though."

"I'm a couples' therapist for your information."

"Well, I hope this is not how you treat your clients."

With one last haughty stare, she exits the office and entrusts the signed lease to Leslie, who stashes it away into the black leather folder she's holding in her arms.

Then, to my utter surprise, they hug.

"Thank you, Lee," the woman in red says. "This space will be perfect for my law practice."

5

"Glad I could help." Leslie smiles, and hands her evil client a set of keys. "These are officially yours."

Sporting a smug smile, the donut thief walks back to the door and pointedly stares me down. I'm still in her office; I've been petrified in here ever since Medusa put her eyes on me. I let out one last, defeated scoff and storm out of her precious private property. She locks the door, gives Leslie another quick side hug, saying, "I'll see you tomorrow." And then she's gone.

The moment the elevator disappears, I ask, "You know that witch?"

"Hey," Leslie says. "Vivian is one of my best friends."

Vivian. So, the Gorgon has a name. "What kind of law does she practice?"

"She's a divorce attorney."

A Marriage Terminator, why doesn't that surprise me?

"I'm sorry she snatched up the corner office," Leslie continues. "But I'm sure we can find you another place."

"Leslie, please tell me you have something decent to show me today, *right now*. I only have a week left to move."

I've only recently switched to Leslie as a real estate agent, since my old agency could not deliver, and it isn't fair to put so much pressure on her, but I'm desperate.

"As it happens"—Leslie shifts the black leather folder to a one-arm hold, and uses her free hand to fish a fresh set of keys out of her bag—"the office next door is still available. But you should know all the lots in this building are going fast."

She unlocks the middle door. "Not a corner office like you wanted, but it's spacious and bright."

I follow her inside and assess the space. Not bad. The

back wall is made of windows, in the same distressed metal and glass theme I've seen around the entire building, and light pours in, leaving no dark corners. Still, compared to the office next door, this is a poor facsimile.

I close my eyes to remove from my mind any memory of the adjoining space. Instead, I concentrate on all the sad hovels I've visited in these past few months. When put into perspective, it's a no brainer.

"I'll take it," I say to Leslie.

"Really? Wonderful! Sign the papers, and the lease is yours. You can move in right away. And, good news—the rent is lower for this office."

I would've gladly forked over the extra bucks for the corner office, but let's concentrate on the positives. Except for the questionable neighbor, this place is perfect.

Two

Vivian

Freight elevator. I'm not a fan of this feature of my new office building. Slow, lumbering... But at least they're spacious enough that Tegan and I can move all my stuff upstairs in one journey. Hiring a moving company would've been easier, but those are expensive, and I have a specific storing system. I couldn't risk them messing up my files. So, elbow grease it is.

"Mom," Tegan wines as she hauls one of the last boxes into the elevator. "You promised today would be fun."

"We're almost done, honey," I say. "And then we can go get ice cream like we do every Saturday."

She drops the box to the elevator floor, still with the long face. "I'm not five anymore, you know?"

Don't I? At fifteen, my daughter is in that weird phase of life where she's not yet a woman but is no longer a kid. But to me, she'll always be my baby. And we're going to keep the tradition of Saturday morning ice creams alive for as long as she'll allow it—even under protest.

"Wait here," I say, heading for the front doors that lead out to the street. "And make sure the elevator stays put."

Before exiting, I pause, checking behind my shoulder to see if Tegan has blocked the doors like I asked. And there she is, leaning against the doorframe in her faded jeans, white sneakers, and a flannel shirt. Dark-blonde hair loose on her shoulders, arms crossed over her chest, and a slight frown complete the teenage-fantastic look.

I tear my eyes from my sulky daughter and quickly cross the street to where I've parked the small truck we rented for the big move today. But instead of one, I find two identical trucks parked next to each other. I'm not even sure which one is mine, until I spot the driver still behind the wheel of the truck on the left. The man is tall, even sitting down, with a distinctive mop of curly dark hair, blazing blue eyes, and a chiseled face that'd be hard to forget. He's the crazy guy who barged into my new office two days ago, a minute after I'd signed the lease, accusing me of everything that ever went wrong with his life.

What is he doing here?

Keeping to the side opposite of him, I close the distance to my van. Let's hope he won't spot me so I can dodge another unpleasant exchange. Also, I don't want him to see me in jeans, sneakers, and an old sweater. When I go into battle, I prefer to wear my lawyer armor, and for my shoes to be *spikey*. Especially because the fool must've decided it'd be a good idea to move offices while wearing another impeccably tailored suit—navy blue like the one he had on the other day. Rude *and* impractical. What an idiot.

Luck isn't on my side, though.

The moment I unlock the rental vehicle and its lights blink to life, the man rolls down his window and yells, "Hi, hello, sorry to bother you, but I'm stuck. I can't open the door enough to get out. Could you please move your truck to the left a little? You have space."

I pick up the last box from the rear of the van and circle back to the front, this time walking directly into his line of sight. "Sorry," I say, watching with gusto as his blue eyes widen in recognition. "But I have an elevator full of boxes and I can't keep it busy all morning."

A flash of challenge blazes across his eyes, but it quickly disappears. He must have realized he can't yell at me again and expect me to do him a favor. Time to eat some humble pie, Mr. Stuck.

His Adam's apple bobs up and down in one dismayed swallow.

Ah, bet that pill tasted bitter.

True to expectations, his voice is polite-verging-on-pleading as he speaks next. "Please, it'd only take you a minute to move the truck."

"Sorry," I repeat, using my most civil tone. "I can't help you. But I'm sure you can find another parking spot somewhere."

I turn on my heel and stroll back into the building, not sparing the man a second glance. Guess he should've thought about paying it forward with kindness before he started asking for favors. What goes around *always* comes around, buddy.

"What took you so long?" Tegan accuses the moment I drop the last box on top of all the others.

"Nothing, honey, we're good to go," I say, pushing the button to the third floor.

The ride takes forever, and when the doors finally open, I place a big box in the middle to keep them from closing. Without wasting time, Tegan and I begin hauling boxes out of the elevator and into my new office. I only need to move everything inside today; I'll come back tomorrow alone to sort and organize. I'll also have to put together the new furniture, which came in suspiciously tiny packages that promise an assembling hell.

We're halfway through the moving when an Indian woman clad in all black—jeans, sweatshirt, beanie—with combat boots to match comes up the stairs, panting. She can't be much older than Tegan; twenty-three to twenty-five, tops, would be my guess.

"Oh, that's why the elevator isn't working," she says.

"Hi, sorry," I reply. "I'm trying to make it as quick a job as possible."

See? I'm already disrupting the building's services as it is. I couldn't have possibly kept the elevator locked any longer to move the truck.

And why am I still thinking about that man and his problems?

I'm not. He couldn't be further from my thoughts.

"You must be our new neighbor," she says, extending a hand. "I'm Indira. Nice to meet you."

I shake her hand. "Vivian Hessington. Nice to meet you, too. This is my daughter, Tegan."

Tegan gives Indira that cool, indifferent nod that all teenagers seem to have perfected.

"You gals need help?" Indira offers.

"No, thank you, I wouldn't want to trouble you."

"No trouble at all," Indira assures me. "I only came in on a Saturday because I forgot my phone charger last night. I'll grab it real quick and be back in a sec," she adds, and then disappears through the wide metal and glass doors opposite to my office.

Two minutes later, she joins Tegan and me in moving boxes, chairs, and filing cabinets.

"Seems like today is the official move-in day for half the building, uh?" Indira says between runs.

"What do you mean?" I ask.

"Another guy down in the lobby is hauling in a bunch of boxes. He was waiting for the elevator, too, I think."

My heart sinks. It doesn't take a genius to figure out that horrible man must've rented a space in this building. All the dots line up. That basket case wanted my office, and Lee is his real estate agent. Plus, what else would he be doing here with an ill-parked moving truck?

I eye the middle door suspiciously. Let's hope he's at least on another floor.

I've just carried the last box out of the elevator when my unspoken wish is crushed, as Mr. Impractical comes up the stairs with a carton box in his hands. Our eyes meet across the landing, and he gives me the stare of death. I glare right back at him, waiting until he drops his gaze.

Men, I've found, can be a lot like wolves; you have to show them who the alpha is right away.

Mr. Blue Eyes struggles to get his keys out of his pants pocket while holding the box in his hands, until after a few long seconds, he comes to the obvious conclusion that he should drop the box first, and then open the door. He's finally turning the key in the lock when Tegan shuffles out of my new office, calling, "Are we done yet, Mom?"

The man's hand stops mid-motion, and I witness the usual reaction take place on his face as he turns to me. His eyes and mouth widen in surprise at finding out I have a teenage daughter, and then a small frown appears as he no doubt starts making calculations.

She must've been barely eighteen when she had her, I can practically hear him thinking.

Nineteen, for your information, I silently snap inside my

head.

To his credit, he's quicker than most to hide the shock and compose his features back to normal.

Indira comes out of my new office next, defusing whatever unspoken tension has passed between me and that man. "You're on this floor, too!" she says to him with a wide smile. "We're finally a complete family. Great, we were getting lonely all by ourselves here on third." She points at her office.

The man finishes unlocking his door and then moves closer to us, offering his hand to Indira.

"Dr. Lucas Keller," he says.

What a tame name for someone with such a bad temper.

They shake hands, and he does the same with Tegan next. When my turn comes, he pointedly drops the friendly hand to his side.

Both Indira and Tegan stare at us questioningly, so I explain, "We've met already."

Lucas nods, acknowledging our mutual dislike once again with the downturn of his mouth.

"I'd better get a move on." He waves politely at the other two and goes back to his box, bending ninety degrees to pick it up and regaling the three of us with a view of white men's boxer shorts peeking through a tear in the backside of his pants.

Indira is the quickest to recover. "Hey, Luke, not sure if you know, but you've ripped your pants. We can see the whole jolly family from over here."

Lucas' first reaction is to stand up abruptly and ridiculously turn in half circles while trying to catch sight of his bum and failing miserably. The next step, however, is to glare at me.

Oh, I'd like to see how he's going to blame this on me.

Lucas promptly explains, "I must've ripped them while exiting my van *through the window* because someone refused to move her truck and let me get out the normal way."

All sugar and sweetness, I say, "Perhaps you ought to learn how to park before you rent a truck." I give his preposterous suit a quick once-over. "Or wear more practical clothes when engaging in manual labor."

Dr. Keller just stands there gaping at me, rage simmering in those strikingly blue eyes.

"Come on, Tegan," I quickly add, before this can turn into another heated argument. "Let's go get that ice cream."

I lock my door and call for the elevator that has wandered to some other floor in the meantime. Tegan and Indira wait by my side.

"It was nice to meet you," Lucas says, addressing his remark to them, and then disappears inside his hole.

Why, of all the possible office neighbors, did I have to end up next to a grumpy ogre? By the time I come into work on Monday, he'll probably have riddled the landing with wooden "Stay Out" and "Beware Ogre" signs like Shrek. I imagine his face all green and laugh to myself as I enter the elevator and push the ground floor button. Lucas Keller might look nothing like an ogre, but he sure behaves like one. Maybe he's a reverse Shrek: handsome on the outside and ugly on the inside.

"The new neighbor is pretty easy on the eyes," Indira comments.

Ah, she's noticed. Good thing I've had an early show of

his awful personality and can't be fooled by the handsome face.

I shrug at the comment, indifferent.

But Indira insists, "Maybe a bit too old for me; I steer clear of anyone above thirty." And she eyes me suggestively.

How did she guess I'm single? Is it written on my forehead in big letters?

"I'm not looking for a relationship," I say.

Especially not with entitled egomaniacs, I add in my head. But there's no need to share my opinion on the man in question, since Indira has already ruled him out due to old age.

Aha. Bite the bullet, Mr. Ripped Pants.

Three

Lucas

Monday morning, I'm all settled into my new office and have opened up shop. This office, besides being more affordable, is also smaller than my previous one. But since my beloved secretary, Agatha, retired, I've switched to a virtual assistant, saving money and space. Like most New Yorkers, I've had to cut square footage down to the bones. It's the philosophy of this entire building, with a shared concierge and communal waiting area on the ground floor.

My first clients are the Newmans, a couple in their late thirties who I'm meeting for the first time. From how they've been talking to each other so far, I'll be seeing a lot more of them in the upcoming weeks.

"You know, Doctor," Mr. Newman says, "that women on average use three times as many words as men."

"We shouldn't make this a battle about gender," I say, as Mrs. Newman rolls her eyes and retorts, "That's because we have to constantly repeat ourselves!"

"Oh, sorry," Mr. Newman snaps, "it must be my brain filtering you out in a valiant attempt to protect me from your yapping orders all day long." He mimics the blah-blah-blah hand gesture. "Yap, yap, yap."

"How? You're never around," Mrs. Newman seethes, then turns to me. "You know what he does, Doctor? He pretends he has to work late every night, but I know he's lying. He can't be having a crisis every single day, it doesn't make sense. Unless he's having an affair, of course. Last week, I called his secretary, and she said he'd left already, but he didn't come home until two hours later. No traffic is that bad."

Mr. Newman completely disregards the accusation and stares at me with a satisfied grin. "See, Dr. Keller, I won this one." He makes the hand gesture again. "Yap, yap, yap... It never ends."

I take a deep breath. "Mr. Newman, this isn't about winning. You and your wife are on the same team. If she loses, you lose, too. Part of counseling is to go back to a win-win mentality. But before we can do that, we need to re-establish trust. Mr. Newman, please respond truthfully: Are you having an affair?"

The husband scoffs, clearly offended. "No."

I sigh in relief. Without a third person involved, my job will be a lot easier.

"Okay," I say. "Are you pretending to work late to avoid being at home?"

He hesitates.

"Please be honest," I encourage. "This is a safe space to share."

He nods. "Yes."

His wife turns on him, mouth gaping open, ready to attack, but I silence her with a raised hand.

"Thank you for being forthright, Mr. Newman. Now we finally have a starting point. Could you please explain to us, in your own words, why you don't want to spend time at home?"

Mr. Newman shifts uncomfortably in his chair. "Whenever I'm in the house, I'm either treated like the handyman or an unwanted guest. We never talk about

17

anything interesting anymore. I wouldn't even know why she'd want me home."

"Why would you feel like an unwanted guest?" Mrs. Newman asks.

"You're always busy running after the kids, and never pay me any attention—"

"That's not true—"

"All right," I say. "Let's put a pin in the discussion. The issue is clear, and the good news is, it's fixable. To start, I want you both to think about an activity you enjoyed doing together when you first met."

The troubled couple considers my request for a few moments, until Mrs. Newman says, "Art. We could spend hours talking about an exhibition when we were in college."

"Art, great." I smile. "That's fantastic. Starting this week, I want you to institute an artistic date night. Visit the Met, pick a floor, a time period, and go to dinner afterward. Just the two of you, phones off."

"What if something happens to the kids?" Mrs. Newman asks.

"If you prefer not to turn off your phone, then put it on 'do not disturb.' Set your home number or the babysitter's as the only calls that can get through."

"I can do that?" Mrs. Newman mustn't be very techy. "How?"

"I can show you," I offer.

"No need, Doctor, I can teach her later," her husband says. Look at them—already working together, and they haven't even left my office yet.

"Great," I say, and peek at the clock mounted on the wall behind the Newmans. "I'm afraid our time has run out."

We all stand up, and I escort them to the door.

At the landing, I stop on the threshold while they call the elevator.

"Art date night," I repeat. "Let's try it out, and next week we can discuss how it went."

We say our goodbyes, and I go back to my desk to write a few notes while the session is still fresh in my mind.

But I haven't sat down for five minutes when a riot starts outside.

"Diana! DIANA!" a man is shouting. "Let me see her!"

I get up again and poke my head out on the landing to find a bald guy with a flourishing mustache, dressed in a tweed suit, knocking desperately on the corner office's door.

"Excuse me," I say. "What is all this racket?"

The man points at the door. "She's forbidding me to see my wife."

As if he'd used the magic summoning words, the door flies open and The Wicked Witch of the West Office emerges in the flesh. "I'm not preventing anyone from doing anything, Mr. Cavendish," she says coldly. "Your wife doesn't want to see you."

Ms. Vivian Hessington, Esquire, is back to wearing a skirt suit—burgundy today, pencil skirt as tight as ever—high heels, and that severe bun on top of her head; must be her lawyer uniform. I preferred her in the casual clothes of the weekend—correction, I don't prefer her in any guise, because she's the most aggravating woman in the world.

"Of course," I scoff. I should've known she was responsible for the commotion.

Medusa turns the stare of death on me. "Found good parking today?" She doesn't leave me time to reply before she returns her attention to the poor bastard she's torturing. "Mr. Cavendish, it is useless to bring reinforcements." She pointedly stares at me. "The cavalry won't help you."

"No, listen." I raise my hands. "I'm not involved. I was trying to *work* in my office when this pandemonium started."

She ignores my comment and crosses her arms on her chest. "Mr. Cavendish, unless you want me to ask for a restraining order, I suggest you leave."

"A restraining order? But for what? I just want to talk to my wife. Diana, Diana, I'm sorry. I love you."

From somewhere inside the corner office, his wife mumbles, "He sounds sincere."

The witch's nostrils flare. "He only wants to pay less alimony, trust me, Mrs. Cavendish."

"No," the man insists. "I don't want to pay any alimony, because I don't want a divorce."

Mr. Cavendish really does sound sincere, so, despite my better judgment, I get involved. "Let them talk," I suggest. "If there's a chance they could resolve their issues, why prevent it?"

Medusa crosses the hall to the elevator and pushes the call button. "There's no chance," she says. "Mrs. Cavendish has decided."

Once the machine arrives, she opens the metal grate door, showing the poor man the inside. "Now, I suggest you leave, Mr. Cavendish, this is private property. Unless you want me to add stalking to the list of grounds for the proceedings."

The dejected husband is ready to give up, when I once again intervene. "No need to leave, Mr. Cavendish. You're my guest, you're not trespassing."

He falters on the elevator doorstep.

"Get in," the witch orders, "or I'll have no choice but to call the police."

So it isn't just me; Medusa likes to terrorize everyone. To hell with the police and the private property. This is now equally about helping Mr. Cavendish and sticking it to Miss High-And-Mighty.

The threat, however, is enough to scare the poor bastard for good, and he gets into the elevator. And since I'm already too invested in the drama, I follow him inside. "Mr. Cavendish, why don't you come to my office and explain the situation to me, and we can see if we might find a solution."

While I'm distracted with talking, the witch reaches inside and pushes the Lobby button. Medusa pulls the grate door closed, setting the elevator in motion.

I glare at her, and she gives me a one-handed goodbye wave, smirking with satisfaction as we disappear into the bowels of the building.

There's no way I'm giving up that easily. I push the stop button. The freight machine bumps to a halt between floors. I push the third-floor button, but nothing happens. Uh oh.

Mr. Cavendish's breath turns ragged as he asks, "It isn't working?"

He looks pale and sweaty and is rolling a finger inside the collar of his dress-shirt as if to loosen it.

"Are you claustrophobic, Mr. Cavendish?"

"Yes. No. A little."

***

Mr. Cavendish ends up being carried away on a stretcher forty-five minutes later, still in the throes of a claustrophobia-induced panic attack. After the elevator stopped, I had to call the building superintendent to come free us, and it took a while.

The paramedics carry Mr. Cavendish into an ambulance and perform a few basic checks. Meanwhile, I sag on a bench outside the building, tilt my face up to the sun, and close my eyes for a second.

A click to my right makes me blink and turn toward the source of the noise. The teenage daughter of the Wicked Witch of the West Office has sat down beside me and is holding a pale pink Polaroid camera in her hands.

"Hi," I say.

"Hey," she says back, and, jerking her chin toward the now-departing ambulance, she asks, "Did Mom do that?"

"Why? People often leave her office on a stretcher?"

The daughter flashes me a wide, wicked-but-candid grin that I could imagine mirrored on her mother's face if the woman *ever* smiled.

"Only the male kind," she says.

I shake my head and smile back. "You don't seem as prejudiced against my gender. Tegan, is it?"

She nods, then shrugs. "I'd better go. We're supposed to have lunch together, and I don't want to be late or Mom will go ballistic."

That gives me pause. "Shouldn't you be in school?"

"Today's a half-day. The teachers hold this meeting once a year on how to be better at their jobs."

"That sounds like a great initiative."

"It sucks. The great project usually adds up to two weeks full of stupid, newfangled teaching methods that don't work and will be dropped in no time. But, hey, I got to skip Calculus, so I'm not complaining."

"Really?" I laugh. "What was the weirdest thing they made you do?"

Tegan's lips curl up. "Last year, Mrs. Robison decided we should all cosplay Shakespeare to get us more involved... But, like, not just in class. In real life. Bunch of teenagers walking around dressed in 15th century clothes... Didn't last long, let me tell you." She shrugs and stands up. "I gotta go now."

"I'll walk in with you," I say, getting up from the bench. Can't buy lunch if I don't have my wallet, which I inconveniently left on my desk upstairs.

In the lobby, I eye the elevator suspiciously. After spending nearly an hour locked in that cage, I'm not keen on repeating the experience. No matter how "fixed" the superintendent claims the elevator now is.

So, with a friendly nod, I leave Tegan in front of the grate doors, saying, "I'll take the stairs."

She waves goodbye, showing more friendliness in her pinkie than the sum of her mother's entire being.

In my office, I find my laptop still open on my session notes. Right. In all the excitement, I'd nearly forgotten about the Newmans. I'd better finish the notes before I take my lunch break.

Unfortunately, as I sit at the desk, my brain refuses to concentrate on the Newmans. It keeps going back to the woman next door and her daughter.

Tegan must be fifteen or sixteen—which, unless her mother has an excellent plastic surgeon, means Medusa must've had her when she was a teen. Eighteen, nineteen at max.

I wonder if there's a father in the picture. From the brief

interaction I witnessed on Saturday, their dynamic spoke of a consolidated duo. I'd bet my right hand there's no dad. Why? What happened? Is that why Miss Attorney has such a bone to pick with men?

My phone rings, interrupting my musings. It's Garrett, my best friend.

"Hey, buddy, what's up?" I ask.

"Luke, I did it! I asked Leslie to marry me last night. We're engaged!"

"Whoa, man, congratulations!"

"Thanks, dude, it was a long time coming. And you were right, it was stupid to be scared. Leslie is my best friend and I'm lucky to have her."

Garrett has been hinting he might propose for months now, but I thought he was still too terrified of commitment to actually pop the question. Apparently not.

"Want to grab a beer tonight, celebrate?" I ask.

"Yeah, man. But we're also hosting an informal engagement party Saturday night at our house. You're coming, right?"

"Sure, what time?"

"Six. Sorry, Luke, gotta bounce, lot of calls to make. Catch you later at the Full Shilling?" he asks, naming our favorite pub for after-work drinks. "Usual time?"

"Perfect, later, man," I say, and hang up.

Garrett is like a brother to me, and I'm thrilled his relationship with Leslie has hit such an important milestone. Still, I can't help feeling a little wistful, and my mind inevitably drifts to Brenda. My ex-girlfriend of two years, who was offered a promotion in Chicago six months ago and didn't even bother to ask me if I'd consider moving before she packed up and left. New job, new life, new boyfriend, probably.

It was a blow, not gonna lie. I pride myself on being good at reading people, and always preach to my clients to be attentive to their partners' feelings. With Brenda, I failed on both counts. I was blind to what was going on in my backyard. Which has led to another instance of me not practicing what I preach. I haven't been on a date ever since Brenda left me. I've refused all subtle and not-so-subtle offers from my parents—mostly Mom, admittedly—and friends to set me up with that perfect relative/friend/vague acquaintance they just knew I'd hit it off with. Online dating isn't for me, too prosaic. And I haven't met anyone the old-fashioned way. But Garrett's announcement has stirred a dormant longing. Life is short. I shouldn't waste it pining after someone who tossed me aside with no regrets. Time to move on. Yeah, I might be ready to jump back on the proverbial horse.

Right, next time someone offers to set me up on a date, I vow to keep an open mind.

Four

Vivian

What an awful first day at the new office. This morning, that Cavendish mess. Then, in court, the hearing before mine dragged on forever, bungling my afternoon schedule and forcing me to pull long hours to get everything on track for tomorrow.

As a result, I get home super late and well past dinnertime. The house is silent, meaning Tegan must be in her room with her headphones on. Before saying hello to my daughter, I hop into the bathroom real quick to change into more relaxing clothes.

In front of the mirror, I let loose my hair from the tight bun I keep it in while at work and massage my scalp with my fingers. After a day wrapped up so tightly, it's a mess. I drop the pins and donut styler in the drawer under the sink and comb through the rat's nest with a brush. Unable to resist, I check the tips and pull off a few split ends. I should probably stop abusing my hair like this, but I've been in the Mom Bun Club since Tegan was born, and now I'm addicted to not having to deal with hair in my face or, heaven forbid, actually have to style my locks. The curling iron at the bottom of the drawer stares up at me accusingly. I haven't used it in—how long? I couldn't say, but the thin layer of dust covering the handle is a clear hint it's been too long.

I drop my burgundy suit and cream blouse in the dry-cleaning laundry basket and move to my bedroom to change into a pair of leggings, an oversized sweater, and comfy socks.

Once I'm settled in my cozy gear, I knock on Tegan's door.

There's no answer.

And, okay, moms aren't ever supposed to—under no circumstances—enter their teenagers' sacred bedrooms without the occupant's express permission, a warrant, or at least probable cause. But Tegan is a sweet kid, and she's probably just listening to music too loud to hear me. So, I do the unthinkable and turn the knob.

True to expectations, my daughter is on her bed, laptop on her legs, giant headphones covering her ears while she bounces her head up and down in rhythm to a tune. Our cat, Priscilla, is nestled between the pillows of Tegan's queen bed where she knows she shouldn't sleep. The covers are fair game, but the pillow area is forbidden, which, in our cat's mind, must be exactly the appeal.

I sit at the foot of the bed, causing Tegan's head to snap up and her eyes to go wide as she shuts the laptop at the speed of light.

What was she doing?

Unfortunately, I know the rules and am not allowed to ask. I sigh inwardly, missing the days when she was little and her biggest life's goal was to spend as much time in my arms as she could. But, alas, those times are gone. Let's focus on the present.

"Hi, honey."

She removes the headphones, nestling them around her neck. "Hey, Mom."

As expected, her tone isn't angry. Tegan doesn't begrudge me the intrusion. And other than shutting her laptop, she welcomes me with a warm smile.

"Did you have dinner already?" I ask.

"Yeah, I ordered pizza. I left you some."

I want to say eating fast-food every night isn't a smart choice, but what right do I have when I wasn't home to make her a healthier meal? The usual inner battle between providing the best financial support for my kid—ensuring Tegan has a solid college fund and can choose whatever school she wants—and the need to be more present in her life rages in my chest. Unfortunately, becoming a parent didn't happen with an instruction manual on what to prioritize.

At least Tegan had a half-day today, and we had a healthy lunch at the salad bar near my new office. If nothing else, she ate some of her vegetables. And for tomorrow night, I'll make the dinner order myself—sushi, or a noodle soup.

And to be honest, I could use leftover pizza right now.

I ask my next standard-issue, end-of-day question. "How was the rest of your day?" And prepare myself for the equally standard non-answer.

It promptly arrives. "Great."

"Did you do anything fun?" I prod.

Tegan shrugs. "Just homework and practice."

She plays varsity volleyball.

When it's clear I'm not getting any further information out of her unless I switch into interrogation mode, I smile and lean down to kiss the side of her head. "Okay, honey. I'm going to eat and watch some TV. I'll be in the living room if you want to hang out." She probably won't, but I always extend the offer, just in case.

Half a pizza later, I settle on the couch ready for a good movie. I grab the remote and am about to turn on the TV when my phone rings.

"Lee! Hey."

"Hi! How's the new office treating you?"

"It's perfect. Thank you again for setting me up. I couldn't have wished for anything better." *Ogre neighbor excluded,* my brain adds. "What's going on with you? How was your weekend?"

A long, happy sigh comes through the line.

"Garrett proposed last night," Leslie says, and my stomach drops.

"Wow, that's amazing," I say, trying to infuse enthusiasm in my tone. Don't get me wrong, I'm happy for Leslie—but, lately, everyone around me is dropping off the single list right and left. In my twenties, it was okay to be on my own. I had as many unattached friends as I wanted. But now that I'm approaching thirty-five, that is no longer the case. I can count the people I know who aren't married or engaged on the fingers of one hand. Leslie is the perfect example: we met four years ago at a Pilates class, both single, and now she's engaged.

After years of practice, I'm trained on all the questions I should ask next, so I fire them all at once. "Were you expecting it? How did Garrett ask? Send me a picture of the ring."

"Wait a second." Scuffling noises replace Leslie's voice, no doubt as she lowers the phone to forward me the perfect ring shot she must've already sent to all the people she called with the happy announcement.

A second later, my phone chimes with an incoming text. I stare, mesmerized, at a close up of Leslie's hand with the Manhattan skyline in the background. On her ring finger shines a majestic pear cut diamond—over one carat, of the purest quality—that must've cost Garrett a small fortune.

For someone who gave up dating a long time ago, I'm becoming quite the expert on engagement rings.

"It's beautiful," I say. No need to infuse fake admiration in my voice—it's gorgeous. "How did he ask?"

"Oh, he completely blindsided me. We were going on our usual run Sunday night. Garrett timed it so we'd reach Brooklyn Bridge Park at sunset, and then pretended he had to stop to tie his shoe. He dropped to one knee, pulled out the ring, and popped the question." Leslie chuckles. "I should've been suspicious; he sent me to a manicure appointment Saturday I couldn't remember booking."

A sneak manicure. A small thing compared to a proposal. But Garrett knows how much Leslie cares about her Instagram, and he made sure she could take the perfect engagement photo with perfectly lacquered nails. Gosh, what it must be like to have someone care for and love you that much.

My chest tightens.

Hoping my voice isn't too strained, I say, "I'm so happy for you, Lee. Have you already picked a date?"

"We're thinking of summer next year. That should give me enough time to plan for everything."

That's when the jealous, cynic, scorned woman in me takes over for a second. "Don't forget to come to me for a prenup first."

"Sheesh, Vivi, romantic much?"

I rein in my inner bitter bitch and hastily apologize. "Sorry. It's just the lawyer in me talking. You know I can't help it. I'm sure you and Garrett won't need a prenup."

Leslie lets out a nervous laugh. "I hope not."

An awkward silence follows, so I break the tension by asking a silly question. "Have you already bought all the bridal magazines on Earth?"

"Not yet." I can hear the easy smile return in Leslie's voice. "But I might have abused Pinterest a little."

"Oh, gosh, that must've been quite the rabbit hole."

"Yep, I have to delete the app from my phone, it's a drug. Uh, listen, anyway, Garrett and I are hosting an informal engagement party Saturday night at our house. Are you free?"

"Sure," I say.

"Great, I'll text you the details."

We hang up, and I stare around the living room for a few seconds, at a loss for words. A familiar lump in my throat is lodged in place, no matter how many times I try to swallow it away.

How did I end up here? In my mid-thirties, with no love life to speak of, and no prospect of a relationship. I'm a romantic at heart, but fifteen years of bad relationships have kept telling me I'm wrong. First, with what happened with Tegan's father. Then, with all the gruesome love-turned-to-bitter-resentment I witness daily in my job. And, finally, with a good chunk of the men in New York not interested in dating a single mom. But when did I stop trying? I can't even remember the last date I went on. Still, stories like Leslie's make me hope love is possible, even in this chaotic world.

Not if you don't put yourself out there, a voice admonishes in my head.

Garrett didn't just fly into Leslie's lap; she actively pursued a relationship.

Right, they met through a dating agency. I always thought that having an algorithm choose my life's partner wouldn't be romantic, but…

I pull up Leslie's engagement ring photo again. What's not romantic about this? Nothing, it's perfect. What does it matter how they met? Zilch. Nada. Maybe I should ask Leslie the name of the agency… An irrational fear makes me shudder at the mere suggestion. One day… We'll see.

I grab the remote and turn on the TV, shuffling channels until the screen shows Demi Moore and Patrick Swayze making pottery. I drop the remote on the coffee table and wrap myself in a blanket. A *Ghost* re-run is just the heartbreaking kind of movie I need tonight.

Tegan finds me a while later, unabashedly crying to the notes of *Unchained Melody*.

"*Ghost*, Mom?"

I look up at her, wiping a few tears off my cheeks. "I couldn't resist."

She sighs and shakes her head. "We need ice cream for this. Vanilla, or the heavy stuff?"

Our eyes lock, and we nod, saying in unison, "The heavy stuff."

When she comes back from the kitchen with two bowls of chocolate chip cookie dough ice cream, I lift the blanket and pat the empty spot on the couch next to me. Tegan scoots right in, snuggling close to me under the blanket, filling my heart with love. Five seconds later, Priscilla joins us, curling up between us. I scratch the cat behind the ears, and she begins to purr.

Who said I need a man? Maybe my daughter and our cat are enough.

Said the sad lady who cries watching decades-old romantic fantasy thrillers.

***

Wednesday morning, at the office, I drum my fingers on the desk anxiously. I hate it when a client is late. My calendar is precise, scheduled, organized down to the minute. And, no, I'm aware not everyone is as punctual or efficient as I am, so I always keep a half hour buffer between appointments. But Mrs. Thomas is now officially forty-five minutes late. I sure hope she won't show up now, expecting me to still receive her.

Well, her separation papers are ready to go; all that's missing is her signature. I'll FedEx them to her, and she can have them delivered back to me. Couriers, at least, are reliable.

I search for her number in her file and call her.

After the line rings forever, I'm connected to her voicemail.

"This is Mary. I can't pick up the phone right now. Please leave a message and I'll call you right back."

Right back in her vocabulary, as I soon discover, means "Whenever I get around to it." Three days later, on a sunny Friday afternoon, she still hasn't returned my call. Honestly, I'm getting a little worried. Considering how much in a hurry she was to get divorced, you'd think she wouldn't ignore my calls unless she was in trouble or something.

I'm downtown shopping for Garrett and Leslie's engagement present for the party tomorrow night when, what do you know, I spot Mary Thomas herself coming out of *Eataly,* a fancy food store that sells Italian specialties. She

33

has a man on her arm, and they're looking into each other's eyes like two lost love birds. I smile to myself, worries vanishing into the wind. She's not in trouble—she's met someone! In the excitement of her new relationship, she must've forgotten our appointment, or to return my message. Love does that to people.

I watch as he feeds her a spoonful of gelato from his cup.

Yep, definitely two turtle doves.

I hate to crash her date, but if Mrs. Thomas wants to start a new life with that nice man, she'd better put her soon to be ex-husband well and forever in her past.

And I can help her turn that page for good. No matter how unpleasant the task, or how taken by her new relationship she might be, she'll thank me in the end. And since she won't return my calls or show up for her appointments, it seems the only way I can finalize her divorce is to remind her about the missing signature right now, when I have access to her.

I cross the street over to their side, calling, "Mrs. Thomas!"

Mary looks at me and pales. Wait, is she trying to avoid me? Yep, she's steering her companion away, pretending she hasn't seen me. Why? Is it because I know she's still technically married, and she's ashamed of being with someone new before the divorce papers are finalized?

I'm not one to be discouraged easily, so I run after her, still calling, "Mrs. Thomas! Mary Thomas!"

Mary tries to keep going, but the man tugs at her arm, slowing her down so I can catch up with them. As I approach, I hear him saying, "What's wrong? You look so pale."

"I'm fine, I just—" Mary cuts herself off as I reach their side. "Hello," she says warily.

"Afternoon, Mrs. Thomas," I say. "I expected you at my office on Wednesday. Did something happen? I left you a message but never heard from you."

"Oh, right." She's still looking at me with that deer-caught-in-the-headlights scared look, her smile tense. "I should've called you, but this week has been crazy. My dad fell and broke his hip, and my dog got food poisoning."

Even if she's telling the truth, these are nothing but excuses. It takes all of three minutes to pick up the phone and call me. Still, I'm not in the habit of antagonizing my clients, so I move on. "I have your papers ready. All you need to do is sign, and you and your husband—"

"My husband is here," she cuts me off, pulling on the man's arm. "This is Cedric. I've decided to give him a second chance."

My jaw drops, and I stare at the man directly for the first time. I've never met him before, so I didn't recognize him. All Cedric Thomas has ever been to me is a name on a page, a mysterious figure I needed to get my client away from with as little emotional and financial loss as possible.

Mr. Thomas flashes me a big smile. "She came this"—he brings his index and thumb together until they're almost touching—"close to divorcing me. But I can't complain; it's only thanks to her bitch-face of a lawyer that we're back together. If Mary hadn't gone to her, we would've never met the wonderful couples' therapist who works next door. Total chance, Mary and Dr. Keller bumped into each other in the elevator, and he convinced her to give our marriage a second chance. One hour with him put us back on track. Heck." He side-hugs his wife—who by now has gone pale with mortification—and looks down at her adoringly. "We've never been happier."

He pauses, then winces. "Sorry, I just realized how rude I've been, I haven't introduced myself, Cedric Thomas, and you are?"

"Her bitch-face of a lawyer," I snap. "So nice to meet you." Mr. Thomas goes as pale as his wife, and neither says a word. I give them one of the fakest smiles I can muster, then turn on my heel and stride away, leaving them to wallow in their embarrassment.

After a block of speed-walking and venting to myself, I pull out my phone and call Leslie. She picks up on the third ring.

"Vivi. What's up?"

"Hi," I say.

"Are you running? You sound breathless."

"No, just been power-walking all over Manhattan."

"Oh, where are you?"

"Near Madison Square Park."

"Really? I'm three blocks away; you want to meet for a drink?"

I remove my phone from my ear to check the time, and sigh. "No, I can't, I promised Tegan we would have dinner tonight before she goes to the movies with her friends. And I'm also carrying your present for tomorrow night, still unwrapped."

"Hm? Madison Square Park, you said… What special shops are there? I can't think of anything."

"Now, don't you go Google-Earthing the entire block! Be patient until tomorrow night and you'll love the surprise, trust me."

"Okay," Leslie says. "So if you're rushing through

Midtown with secret, unwrapped presents I'm not supposed to know about, why are you calling me?"

"That man you put in the office next to mine—I need him gone."

"Who, Lucas? Why? I know when you met him he seemed a little crazed, but he was stressed about finding a new office and he had his heart set on a corner one. But, usually, he's a nice guy, I swear. Actually…"

"What?" I ask.

"Garrett and I couldn't wait to introduce you guys… We hoped you would, you know, hit it off or something."

I scoff. "With that maniac?"

"He's not—it doesn't matter. Luke probably isn't ready yet, anyway."

I take the bait. "Not ready, why?"

"His last girlfriend walked out on him, a total blindside, no one saw it coming."

Ah, so much for being the greatest couples' therapist of the century. He couldn't even keep his house in order. I store the information of his ass being dumped not that long ago into his file in my brain. I need all the ammunition I can get.

"Boo-hoo!" I say, unmoved. "I'm heartbroken, but I still want him gone."

"Why?"

"You can't put a couples' therapist next to a divorce attorney, Lee! Not a week in, and he's already poaching all my clients."

"Wait, what? I thought you guys operated at opposite ends of the spectrum. How is he stealing your clients?"

"By turning a bitter wife and an unromantic husband into turtle doves after a magic hour with him is how."

"And that's a bad thing?"

"Of course it is! Come on, you really think years of issues can just vanish with a snap of his fingers? The problems are still there, and once his magic spell wears off, the Thomases are going to be right back where they started." I pause, huff, then add, "Not to mention he's stealing my business! How am I supposed to pay for Tegan's college tuition if he keeps brainwashing my clients? You have to kick him out of the building, Lee. Tell me there's a way."

"Afraid not, honey, his contract is as ironclad as yours."

"Are you telling me I have no chance of getting rid of him?"

"No, not unless he goes voluntarily. But I honestly don't see that happening."

We hang up shortly afterward, and I hurry to catch the subway back to Dumbo. On the train, while I'm jostled and tossed around like a pinball, I brood over the Master Puppeteer of Hearts. I have to get rid of him. Shrek can't come on my home turf, steal my clients like it's nobody's business, and expect no retaliation. Nuh-uh, mister, you picked the wrong divorce lawyer to mess with.

Five

Lucas

Saturday evening, I enter Garrett's building—a Williamsburg condo that has a communal rooftop deck with stunning Manhattan and East River views—careful not to tear the paper of the engagement gift I'm carrying.

I greet the doorman with a cheerful, "Hey, Washington, how's it going?"

"Evening, Dr. Keller. Perfect night for a rooftop party. Everyone is already upstairs; you can go right ahead." He inches his chin toward the elevator.

I nod and cross the hall. After a quick ride up, I step out onto the tenth-floor terrace, where cool lounge music fills the air.

"Luke!" Garrett—who's clearly been stationed on welcoming duties—exclaims. He receives me with open arms and hands me a flute of champagne. "Great to see you, buddy."

I struggle for a second to reposition the perhaps too-large present under one arm, and then accept the glass.

"Man, can I drop this somewhere?" I ask Garrett.

"Oh, you didn't need to bring anything," he protests. "But the gifts station is right over here."

He guides me to the left of the elevator and to a table piled with presents, which clearly shows I *should've* bought a gift. I drop the heavy load on a relatively empty corner, hoping the other guests didn't go too fancy with their presents. A Google search assured me engagement gifts should be something small and sentimental.

Without the package, I'm finally free to move. I roll my shoulders and then sip my champagne while checking out the crowd.

"Wow, great party," I say to Garrett, taking in the catered refreshments, hired barman, and vibrantly colored decorations. "Didn't you say it'd be casual?"

Garrett rolls his eyes. "Ah, man, you know Leslie. She started with 'just a few close friends on the roof' and we ended up with, well"—he motions at the surrounding space—"this."

Garrett steers me toward the closest food station, where a woman is filling a plate with hors d'oeuvres, her back turned to us. "Get something to eat," my friend says. "I've got to go welcome the newcomers."

The woman turns, and her hostile brown eyes widen in recognition.

Miss Attorney looks different tonight. Her hair is loose in soft waves that reach to her shoulders, and she's wearing a frilly blue dress, not one of her power suits.

If this was our first encounter, I'd even go as far as saying she's beautiful. But I know better.

"Ah, Vivian," Garrett says. "This is Luke, my best friend."

Medusa's lips curve in a taught smile. "We've met."

"Of course." Garrett swats himself. "Lee found you offices in the same building, right? Well, enjoy, I gotta get welcoming."

Garrett rushes off, and I narrow my eyes at my ill-disposed neighbor. "Thirty-five years without seeing you once, and now a day can't pass without the *pleasure*."

"Oh, the *pleasure* is all mine." Medusa gives me another one of her petrifying stares, then walks away.

Good riddance.

I shuffle through the crowd, eating a few treats, drinking champagne, and making civil conversation with the other guests I know, until Garrett finds me again about forty-five minutes later.

"What do you think?"

I shrug at the surroundings. "Amazing party, man."

"Not about the party." He smacks me playfully. "About Leslie's friend."

"Who?"

Garrett waves a hand before my face. "Have you gone blind? Vivian. She's hard to miss."

Hard to miss, for sure. If I'm being objective, Medusa is one of the most beautiful women I've ever seen. Dark brown hair, big Bambi eyes, and that heart-shaped mouth. Pity the more-than-pleasant appearance doesn't come paired with an equally amiable temperament.

"Yeah, sorry, man, she's not my type."

"Really?"

I study my friend. "You seem hurt by the revelation. What's up?"

Garrett hides half a grin. "Oh, nothing, it's just that she's single, you're single, so Leslie and I thought…"

I scoff, while pocketing the information that, indeed, there's no father in the family picture of my office neighbor.

"You're not seriously trying to play matchmaker, are you?"

"Why not? She's great, you're great… We were just waiting for the right moment to introduce you guys."

I raise an eyebrow. "And by the *right moment,* you mean…?"

Garrett stares out across the East River. "Once you were ready to date again." He turns to look at me. "Are you? It's been six months since Brenda left."

I consider my answer for a second. Not a week ago, I promised myself I'd be more open to friends' offers to match me up.

Not with the Wicked Witch of the West Office, though, a voice protests in my head.

Okay, maybe not her… But someone else? Why not?

"Yeah," I say. "I'm ready."

"That's great, man." Garrett pats me on the shoulder. "Listen, if you don't want to ask Vivian out, you should try the dating agency that set me up with Leslie."

"I said I was ready to try dating again, not search for a wife."

On my other side, Leslie comes up to me, whispering, "Ah, but it is a truth universally acknowledged, that a single man in possession of a good fortune must be in want of a wife."

I shrug. "Get me the good fortune, and then we can talk about the wife."

"Such a material man," a familiar voice comments from behind Leslie.

Garrett's fiancée moves to the side to reveal Medusa in all her wicked glory.

"Oh, please," Leslie says. "Luke is the soppiest romantic man on Earth."

Brown eyes glint with amused malice. "Is he now?"

Leslie tsk-tsks at her friend. "As if you can talk." Then,

turning to me, she adds, "Put Vivi in front of a romantic movie and she'll be crying within five minutes—even if it's a comedy! She might even be more helplessly romantic than you."

My turn to be smug. "Is that so, *Vivi?*" I wouldn't have pegged her as having a romantic bone in her body.

From the petty way Medusa is looking at me, I'm sure she'd be happy to show me her tongue, but, not being a child, she settles for an annoying half-smirk.

"Why were you talking about wives, anyway?" Leslie asks, glancing curiously at her fiancé.

"I was telling Luke he should try our dating agency."

"What a coincidence! Vivi just asked me for their information. You guys should go together." Leslie pauses, and gives us a naughty look. Before we can protest, she grabs Garrett's hand and pulls him away, saying, "Come on, honey, time to open the presents."

And I'm alone with Medusa once again.

"The dating agency's all yours," I tell her. "I wasn't sure I wanted to use it anyway."

"Why?" She stares me down. "Afraid all the women would reject you?"

"Women like me just fine."

"Is that why you're single?"

The question cuts a little too close to the heart, so I get petty in return. "How can you be a helpless romantic when it's literally your job to *destroy* marriages?"

She levels me with a stare that could kill. "When a client comes to me, their marriage has already been destroyed. My *job* is to make sure their partner doesn't take advantage of them during the divorce proceedings, and to secure them the best post-marital life that I can."

"And if you get to terrorize someone in the process, that's just a bonus?"

"What are you talking about?"

"How about that poor man you made almost die of a heart attack the other day, all because he wanted to talk to his wife?"

"You do realize he basically ignored her for ten years, right? Way too little, way too late. Why does it always take you men losing something before you understand how much you care? And, anyway, you broke the elevator, not me. So, technically, it was you who almost gave Mr. Cavendish a heart attack."

I'm about to retort when Garrett shouts my name, distracting me.

"And the next present is from Luke, my best friend!" He grabs the package and hands it to his fiancée for unwrapping. Leslie tears the paper and squeals in delight.

"A custom doormat!" She shows her guests the coir doormat personalized with the plural form of Garrett's surname: The Greens.

"Taking for granted Leslie will take his name?" Medusa comments beside me. "Patriarchal much?"

Again, I'm saved the need to respond by Leslie shouting, "And now a gift from my dear friend Vivi! And not just one, but two presents."

"Overachiever much?" I whisper.

Medusa ignores my jab as our hosts unwrap her gifts. The first is a Polaroid camera identical to the one her daughter has, but in light blue instead of pink.

"This is amazing!" Leslie shrieks in delight. "I want to

take pictures of everyone tonight—thanks, Vivi." The bride-to-be pulls out a few more items from the first box: a carrying case, an album, and two packs of film.

In the meantime, Garrett raises his half of the gift for the crowd to see, revealing a personalized hearts Connect Four game engraved with Garrett and Leslie's first names in the middle.

The gifts are cute. Not that I'd ever tell Medusa that.

"Well," Medusa says. "As *fun* as it's been to get to know you better, I think I'll go."

"Please don't let me deter you."

She grimaces. "See you at the office." Then she pauses and, with an evil little smirk, adds, "Or at the dating agency, assuming you're not too afraid of rejection."

"Oh, please, if I signed up I'd be matched up in no time, and definitely before you."

"I wouldn't be so sure, Mr. Soppy. I could wager to the contrary."

"You want to make the bet real?"

"What do you mean?"

"We both sign up to the agency, and if I find my match first, you give me the corner office." The offer tumbles out of my mouth before I've had the time to consider its soundness.

She studies me intently for a few seconds. "And if *I* win?"

I shrug. "What do you want?"

Medusa narrows her eyes at me. "You move out of the building and I never see you again."

It'd be foolish of me to accept. It took me forever to find this office and I should remind myself how desperate I was by the end... But the smug way this woman is looking at me is just too much for me to handle. My common sense goes out the window, and suddenly all I want to do is beat her.

"Deal," I say. "Winner takes it all."

Medusa smiles sweetly. "I'd start packing up boxes if I were you." She raises her flute at me in a mock cheers motion. After taking a sip of bubbly, she adds, "It's a bet."

Six

Lucas

"Welcome to *Listen to Your Heart,* Mr. Keller," the receptionist at the dating agency—a nice brunette in her late twenties—greets me after I give her my name. "We spoke over the phone earlier, right?"

"Yeah," I confirm. The first thing I did this morning when I arrived at the office was to call the agency and set up an appointment, before I could change my mind.

"I'm glad we could fit you in for a last-minute appointment. Mondays are always busy days," the woman—Teresa, her name tag states—says. "People go out on the weekend, can't find anyone decent to date, and finally take the plunge and sign up with us in the new week."

Or, in my case, they're invited to a friend's engagement party, drink too much champagne, and get riled into potentially gambling away a perfectly suitable workspace by the Wicked Witch of the West Office.

"You'll be meeting with one of our Professional Matchmakers," she says. "We always advise you be open and honest with them—both about yourself, and what you're looking for. Remember: we're here to help *you.*"

Professional Matchmaker, the qualification alone makes me cringe with skepticism. What on Earth made me sign up for a dating agency?

Oh, right. The bet.

Stay focused. You want that corner office. And also to find your soulmate. Right. The office is secondary, but it'd be a nice added bonus.

Teresa taps at her keyboard with lacquered nails for a few seconds, then looks up at me with another big smile. "Your appointment is at one, which is perfect, as you'll need about twenty minutes to fill out this short questionnaire."

Teresa hands me a rigid folder with a bundle of papers clipped on top. *Short,* my ass. The sucker must be at least thirty pages. Teresa gestures at the steel-blue leather chairs lining the lobby. "Please, take a seat wherever you like."

I grab a pen and settle in a chair away from the door and the front desk. No one else is waiting, so I have my pick of spots.

With a sigh, I turn the first page of the questionnaire and set to work. I quickly fill in the general information section—Name, Date of Birth, etc.—and move on.

```
5. What is your current relationship
status?

♡ Never married
♡ Divorced
♡ Separated
♡ Widowed
```

I stare at the question. Already the fact that the agency picked heart outlines in place of regular square checkboxes makes me regret signing up for this circus. I'm half-tempted to get up and leave... but then I'd have to pack up my beautiful new office. I'm a man of my word; I'll honor our deal. So, I stay.

As I tick the "never married" box, I wonder what Medusa will check. Is she a divorcee? How does Tegan's absentee father play into their little family drama?

6. Do you have children?

No

Miss Attorney is going to reply "Yes" to this one. And why do I have to think about her with every single answer I give? *Because she's the competition.* Right, that's the only reason.

7. Aside from any children you or your new partner may already have, would you like to start a new family?

Yes

8. Are you open to dating someone who already has children?

Am I?

Kids complicate relationships, especially if they are somebody else's. Years of couples' counseling have taught me that much. They can antagonize a parent's new partner or—an image of sweet Tegan with her open smile and Polaroid camera flashes before my eyes—be much kinder and welcoming than their evil mothers. Yes, kids can be a nuisance and add a layer of difficulty to a relationship. But I can't help feeling that, for the right person, it'd be worth it.

I write "Yes" and turn another page. The next section is titled: "Tell us a little more about yourself."

9. Are you a morning person or a night person?

♡ Morning person

♡ Night Owl

♡ It depends

I tick "Morning person."

10. How active would you say you are?

♡ Very, staying fit is important

♡ I only exercise because I have to

♡ I don't have much time to exercise, but I'd like to do it more often

♡ I'm a couch potato

Every morning I wake up at six to go run. I tick the first heart.

11. What's your ideal vacation?

From the staggering number of multiple-choice options, I check camping, hiking, sports/activity holiday, mountain location, and adventure break.

12. How do you plan your vacations?

♡ I don't, I pack and go

♡ I meticulously plan and schedule everything

♡ I arrange the dates and transportation, but I leave the rest to the moment

I'm a mix of two and three, but prefer to picture myself as a spur-of-the-moment guy, so I pick the last option.

13. If you had a day off work, what would you do?

I'd wake up nice and early and drive north to enjoy a good hike in the woods with my dog, Max.

14. Do you follow a particular diet?

♡ Omnivore

♡ Vegetarian

♡ Vegan

♡ Pescatarian

♡ Flexitarian

♡ Beegan

♡ Macrobiotic

♡ Paleo

♡ Keto

My eyes boggle at the overwhelming number of choices provided. Some I don't even know what they mean. I check Omnivore and move on.

15. What do you like to watch on TV?

Sports, action movies, the news. I'm not much of a TV watcher, though.

After leafing through four more pages of—frankly useless—multiple-choice questions, I finally reach the last page which, to my horror, is all open-ended questions. Don't tell me they're going to make me write an essay? I thought I was done with those when I got my masters in psychology.

Is the third degree just for my Professional Matchmaker to read, or will potential dates read them, too? Should I try to be funny? Charming? I should've asked Garrett to explain more about this process. Clearly, he did something right, because he and Leslie are perfect for each other. Even if her taste in friends leaves something to be desired.

42. What are three of your best life skills?

I go with a charming and fun answer, just in case.

I wear socks that match—and, no, it's not trivial since I don't buy new socks often, which means I'm in a constant war with my socks-eating washer.

The ability to laugh at myself.

I'm good at helping people. With my job, I can ask a few simple questions and understand what problems a couple is struggling with and I can help them work on their relationship. I love watching people rediscover each other.

43. What is the ONE thing that people DON'T notice about you right away that

you WISH they WOULD?

I'm funny

44. Why do you think you're single?

Ah, good question, even if the answer seems obvious.

I haven't met the right person

And finally, the last question.

45. What is the most important thing in your life?

Love. I want to find a partner for life. Someone to love and cherish and support no matter what and who will always have my back in return.

I've barely put a period on the last answer when the receptionist appears before me.

"Mr. Keller," Teresa says, "if you're finished with your questionnaire, I'd kindly ask you to join Jennifer, your dedicated Dating Specialist. Please follow me."

She leads me to an office, where a blonde woman in her mid-forties—paper-thin and wearing too much makeup and fake tan for my tastes—welcomes me with a bright smile.

"Mr. Keller, what a pleasure to meet you." She takes my questionnaire from Teresa and shows me the empty chair in front of her desk. "It's always wonderful to get to know a new client."

As she sits in her chair, she quickly scans the first and second pages of my Q&A. Once settled behind the desk, she continues. "I see a friend referred you to our agency. Would you mind me asking who?"

"Garrett Green," I answer, wondering if she's going to make me repeat all the answers I spent the last half hour painstakingly writing out.

"Oh, right, he and Leslie made such a delightful couple. How are they?"

"Recently engaged."

"Aww, how wonderful. It always warms my heart to know we fostered such a dream match. Has Garrett by any chance already explained how our bespoke and exclusive matching system works?"

I wish she'd cut back on the sales pitch a little. I've already joined, haven't I?

"No," I say.

"All right. Let me explain our process. First, we're going to study your questionnaire thoroughly and pull profiles of women in our system who might be a good fit for you based on your answers."

"You mean *you* pick the matches? I don't have to look at a database or something?"

"No, Mr. Keller, we leave that approach to online dating agencies or *apps*." She infuses enough disgust in the word "app" to let me know exactly what her opinion is of the Tinders of the world. "The questionnaire you just filled out"—she taps the folder—"might've appeared overlong or silly, but I can assure you it's been the secret to our success."

"Okay," I say, not entirely convinced. "You pull up a potential match, and then what? You show me the other person's profile?"

"No, never. The answers you provided today are solely for the staff's eyes. They'll never leave this office."

I groan inwardly. If I'd known that I wouldn't have put so much effort into the open-ended questions. I mean, what's the point if no one is ever going to read them?

"At what point do I actually meet someone?"

"Once we've selected a potential match, we'll send you on a blind date."

"What? Without even seeing a picture of the other person?"

Jennifer shuffles through my questionnaire until she reaches a specific page. "You stated physical appearance is not a critical aspect for you."

"Well, it isn't, but I thought I'd—"

"We prefer to send our clients to a meeting unbiased. Don't worry, Mr. Keller, we do the legwork for you and only propose compatible dates. It's how our model works, and also why we can offer a partial refund to clients who haven't found a match within five dates. It rarely happens."

Five blind dates. Sounds like my worst nightmare come true. And on top of that, I'm paying for the privilege… and a hefty amount, at that.

Once Jennifer escorts me back to the reception, Teresa is free to make me sign the contract and put a significant dent in my finances.

With a wallet considerably lighter, and in a darker mood than when I arrived, I'm about to leave the agency… when Medusa walks in.

Her eyes immediately narrow as they lock on mine, and her lips curl in a teasing grin. She doesn't even say "hello" before launching into a head-on attack. "You didn't waste any time, I see. Are you that afraid of losing?"

"You're not too far behind."

Medusa advances on me and stops a few inches short so that when she talks again only I can hear. "Yes, I'm eager to find a partner." Being this close to her, I'm able to smell her for the first time. An annoyingly pleasant scent of vanilla and patchouli. "Seeing you gone will be the cherry on my wedding cake." Then, raising her tone to normal once more, she adds, "Have a good day."

"You, too," I snap, and storm out of the agency.

My sole consolation is knowing she'll be stuck answering stupid questions for the next thirty minutes, while I'll be outside enjoying a pleasant walk back to the office in the midday sun.

Seven

Vivian

After that horrible man leaves, I introduce myself to the receptionist, Teresa, who hands me a questionnaire to fill out. I take the rigid folder from her, excited. Surveys are a quirk of mine. I love answering questions. I've probably answered all the personality quizzes on Facebook.

From discovering what Disney princess I am: Belle. To what job I should do: Designer. That was a funny one; I'm the least artistic person I know. To what *Friends* character I am: Rachel, of course. To who my TV boyfriend should be: Jim Halpert from *The Office*. Mmm, I wasn't convinced about that one. I would've preferred to get Jon Hamm from *Mad Men*... which is probably why I'm sitting in a dating agency at age thirty-four. Because I have terrible taste in men, and only go for the bad boys who like to have their fun and then leave me alone with a daughter to raise. But I digress.

I sit in one of the blue leather chairs of the reception area and start working on the agency quiz—err, questionnaire.

```
5. What is your current relationship
status?

♡ Never married
♡ Divorced
♡ Separated
♡ Widowed
```

Oh, how sweet that they picked hearts instead of those boring square boxes for their multiple-choice answers! They're so cute. Still, no matter how nice the lettering, the question stings. I mark "never married" while my chest squeezes with unwanted memories of my nineteen-year-old self. Of the day I went to tell Tegan's father I was pregnant, thinking he'd offer right away to marry me and to build a family together. Guess how that one turned out.

Whatever. Water under the bridge.

I shake the past away and concentrate on the present—*the future*. I'm being insanely optimistic about joining Leslie's agency, but I have a good feeling about this. Love is waiting for me. If my best friend found her future husband this way, why shouldn't I?

I'm here for the right reasons.

Contrary to Shrek, the thought pops into my head. I'm sure the only reason he was here today is because he's obsessed with getting my corner office. Soppy romantic? Don't make me laugh. Whatever poor woman he gets paired with will hopefully call his bluff right away like I did. And besides, good things come to the honest. I'm definitely going to find a match before he does.

Are you? the pessimist in me asks. *New York is saturated with single gals looking for an eligible bachelor. And Lucas is single, has a good job, most certainly doesn't live with his parents... The city is full of great-unmarried women but lacking in great-unmarried men.*

Well, Lucas can't be *that* great if his ex walked out on him. Must be that awful temper of his.

Anyway, enough about Shrek. I'm not here because of him. Okay, maybe I'm here a teeny bit because of him, but only to preserve the business I have built with years of sacrifices. I needed a way to get him to move out, and he offered it to me on a silver plate. It's nothing personal; at least, not for me.

Right, let's move on with the questions.

6. Do you have children?

Yes, I have a teenage daughter, Tegan, she's fifteen.

7. Aside from any children you or your new partner may already have, would you like to start a new family?

Yes, I've always wanted to give Tegan a sibling. I'm only sorry the age gap between them will be so wide.

8. Are you open to dating someone who already has children?

Of course, dating a father would be ideal. I wouldn't have to explain all the difficulties of being a single parent to him, and the family would grow right away. The more the merrier, right?

I turn another page and find more multiple-choice questions. Those are the most fun to answer.

9. Are you a morning person or a night person?

♡ Morning person
♡ Night Owl
♡ It depends

I tick night owl. I always have trouble getting to sleep at night, but once I hit that REM cycle I could stay in bed forever.

10. How active would you say you are?

♡ Very, staying fit is important
♡ I only exercise because I have to
♡ I don't have much time to exercise, but I'd like to do it more often
♡ I'm a couch potato

Mmm, am I a couch potato? I'm not super active, but I would like to exercise more; I just never have enough time in the day. I do walk to work every morning, and try to go places on foot as much as possible—that should count for something, right? I check off the third option.

11. What's your ideal vacation?

A lot of options follow, and I select beach holidays, cruises, vacations for pure relaxation, resorts, and spa breaks. Some of the other options make me cringe. Who would even call "hiking" a vacation?

12. How do you plan your vacations?

♡ I don't, I pack and go

♡ I meticulously plan and schedule everything

♡ I arrange the dates and transportation, but I leave the rest to the moment

I plan everything ahead of time. Going somewhere without an accommodation booked would drive me mad. Spontaneous trips are my idea of hell. I've always imagined such a spur-of-the-moment getaway would end up with me soaked in the rain as I looked for a place to sleep in a random town with all the hotels booked solid. Not my thing. I'm a control freak.

13. If you had a day off work, what would you do?

Stay in bed until late. Order a delivery of croissants and a latte to be consumed, also in bed. Maybe go on a little shopping spree. Dinner at my favorite Italian restaurant in Dumbo and then on to the movies for a good rom-com.

14. Do you follow a particular diet?

Wow, so many options. I check Omnivore but add a little note underneath.

**But l try to steer clear of meat as much as
l can.

I'm about to move on to the next question when I pause, then
re-read all the multiple-choice options. I take out my phone
and look up Flexitarian Diet.

> The Flexitarian Diet is a style of eating that
> encourages mostly plant-based foods while
> allowing meat and other animal products in
> moderation.

I thought the term sounded familiar. Yup, it fits me to a tee.
I go back to question 14, strike out Omnivore and my
postscript note, and simply check Flexitarian.

15. What do you like to watch on TV?

Comedies and romance movies.

The questionnaire goes on for a few more pages until I reach
the last one.

43. What is the ONE thing that people
DON'T notice about you right away that
you WISH they WOULD?

l'm romantic. With the job l do, most people
assume l'm a cynic. But l'm just the opposite.
And, yes, l can destroy an opponent in court,
but that doesn't mean l'm not a sweet person
outside the halls of justice.

44. Why do you think you're single?

l had my daughter when l was young. Things didn't work out with the father and l had to raise her on my own. Well, with my parents' help. But still, having a kid while keeping good grades in college first and law school afterward didn't leave me much free time to date. And once l graduated, l still had to work hard to open my practice and provide a stable and financially secure environment for me and Tegan. But now that Tegan is older and mostly self-sufficient, and with my practice now up and running, l feel l've come to a time in my life where l'm ready and free to search for love again.

45. What is the most important thing in your life?

After my daughter, love.

Eight

Lucas

It's a cloudy Tuesday morning, and I've just said goodbye to the Thomases, a couple I saved from the clutches of Medusa. There's still a lot to work on between them, but I'm hopeful they can figure out how to make their marriage last. I'm just jotting down my final thoughts in their file, when my mobile rings. The screen shows an unknown number with a New York area code. "Hello?"

"Dr. Keller? This is Jennifer, your Dating Specialist from *Listen to Your Heart.*"

"Oh, hi," I say unenthusiastically, I'm terrified she'll summon me back to her office to make me answer another set of silly questions. On a positive note, she's switched from Mr. Keller to Dr. Keller, meaning at least she's read my questionnaire.

"Am I catching you at a bad time?" Jennifer asks. I picture her at her desk with a saccharine smile stamped on her lips, probably unhappy about my scarce keenness.

"No, no. I'm between sessions right now. What can I do for you?"

"Ah, Dr. Keller, the real question is what *I* can do for *you.* I've got good news! Our proprietary algorithm has found a potential match for you. We like to book our blind dates on weekends. Nothing speaks of commitment to the cause of finding a life partner as meeting on the most important evening of the week. What message would a Tuesday date night send, right?" Jennifer chuckles. "Are you free this Saturday?"

I sigh inwardly. The Knicks play on Saturday against the Miami Heat, but I'm sure my Dating Specialist would be even less pleased with me if I told her I'm refusing a date to watch a game. At least it's not a home game. If I had to give up a single night of my seasonal membership to Madison Square Garden, I might've cried.

"Yes, I'm free on Saturday."

"Wonderful. Your match has also confirmed she's available. Our agency's policy is that clients do not share names before meeting. We prefer to avoid social media stalking sprees that could generate false ideas based on what people found online."

"So I'll have absolutely no idea of who this woman is until I meet her face to face?"

"That's right, Dr. Keller. But please trust me when I say I've selected an excellent match for you. And also, the mystery adds to the intrigue, the romance. It's a tested strategy we're confident leads to the best results."

"Okay, but how are we going to recognize one another?"

"Ah, that's easy. We ask all our clients to pick aliases. The name can be something funny, or their favorite character from a book. Your date is Miss Bishop." Is Bishop a famous surname? It doesn't ring a bell. I wonder how she chose it. "Who would you like to be, Dr. Keller?"

"Mr. Ewing," I say, picking my favorite Knicks player of all time.

Jennifer sighs. "Another Knicks fan, I see."

She doesn't sound pleased. Should I have picked something funnier? She caught me off-guard, and Patrick Ewing is the first name that popped into my head. Maybe if they were looking for brilliance, they should have given me more than five seconds to come up with an alias.

"Where are we supposed to meet?" I ask.

"The man chooses; we're a little old-fashioned like that. Miss Bishop has expressed a preference for a cozy restaurant or a casual brunch as venues, but since your date is on Saturday night that cuts out brunch."

If I had known I had a choice, I would've gone for lunch and kept the evening free to watch the game. Next time, I won't be fooled.

"Whenever you've picked a location," Jennifer continues, "make a reservation under your alias and send us the details. We'll let Miss Bishop know the time and place. Please put some thought into the restaurant you pick, Dr. Keller. You don't get a second chance at first impressions."

Her condescension irks me. "This may shock you, Jennifer, but I have been on dates before."

Either she misses the sarcasm, or she's too professional to comment on it. "Then I'm sure Saturday will go swimmingly! We'll be in touch soon, Dr. Keller. Have a wonderful day."

If Garrett hadn't sworn time and time again by their service, I would've already quit the agency.

***

Jennifer might not be my favorite person in the world, but she did have a point: first impressions do matter. I spend the afternoon researching potential dinner venues. I hit all the usual suspects first for reviews: *The New Yorker*, Zagat, and *Time Out*. Then, I dig a little deeper, scrolling through my Facebook and Instagram—an activity I rarely engage with— searching for pictures of curated meals and the inevitable gushing comments about the wonderful food and atmosphere.

I make a list of the five most promising spots, then check out their websites. Multiple backup options are essential. Once a restaurant becomes the craze of the New York crowds, it might be hard to find a free table with only a few days' notice.

I call the first name on my list, Il Buco.

"Hello, Il Buco," a female voice picks up. "How can I help you?"

"Hi, I was looking for a table to book on Saturday night."

"Let me check real quick… How many guests?"

"Two."

"We have a table free at six o'clock, and a couple open around ten. Would either of those times work for you, sir?"

For a moment I'm tempted to book the earlier slot; that way, I could do dinner and get home in time to still catch most of the game. But no matter how skeptical I am about this whole "matchmaking" thing, I can't go on a date half-assed, staring at the clock to check the minutes until the game starts and I can be out of the restaurant. It's just plain rude, and I don't want to be that guy. Besides, Miss Bishop will be the first woman I take out after Brenda left, and if I'm jumping back on the horse, I'd better do it with proper riding boots—metaphorically speaking. Not to mention my office is at stake, and it'd be worth going on an amazing date just to see Medusa sweat a little. Will the agency have already set her up on her own blind date? Poor bastard, he has no idea what—

"Sir?" the woman on the other side of the line prompts me.

"Sorry, those are not ideal times for me. Can I think for a

moment and call you back?"

"Sure, but I suggest you decide fast, because the last free tables might be gone soon."

"I will, thank you."

I hang up and call the second place, which, unfortunately, is booked solid for Saturday night.

The third time's the charm, and I find a perfect eight o'clock table available to book. I make the reservation and fire a quick email to Jennifer. I can't handle two conversations in a day with my Dating Specialist.

Her reply comes in right away.

From: jennifer.h@listentoyourheart.com
To: lucas.keller@aol.com
Subject: Re: Dinner Reservation

Wonderful choice, Dr. Keller, I've heard fantastic things about the Boucherie. I'm sure Miss Bishop will appreciate the care you've put into selecting this location.

I wish you the best of luck with your first date. You can expect to hear from me on Monday to collect your feedback on the night and receive Miss Bishop's impressions of you.

And remember, true love is just one date away...

Yours,
Jennifer

Jennifer Harlow
Listen to Your Heart Dating Specialist since 2005

Garrett had better be right about the agency, because I'm feeling a strong urge to kick him in the butt at the moment.

Nine

Vivian

"It's been a pleasure working with you, Mrs. Parker," I say, as I get up to walk my client to the door. "Or should I say, Miss George?"

Her eyes light up. "Miss George, please," she says. "I can't wait to go back to using my maiden name."

"Well, now that the divorce is final, we can certainly make that happen. I'll submit the paperwork for you and send word as soon as the name change goes through."

"Wonderful."

We shake hands, and I walk her out of the office.

The landing is clear, with no signs of the client-poaching monster next door. I wait for Miss George to get into the elevator, then hurry back to my desk where my phone is angrily vibrating.

The number of Tegan's school flashes onscreen, making my stomach drop in a panic. The school never calls unless something is wrong. Did Tegan get hurt? Is she sick?

Heart pounding in my chest, I pick up. "Hello?"

"Miss Hessington?"

"Yes?"

"This is Abel Wentworth, Head of School at The Ignatius College for the Talented and Gifted. I'm calling about your daughter—"

"Did something happen?" I interrupt. "Is Tegan okay?"

"Your daughter is fine, Miss Hessington. I'm reaching out about a matter of… ah… *disciplinary* nature."

Disciplinary? I must've heard wrong. In ten years of schooling, Tegan has never had a single detention. Has the dreaded teenage rebellion phase I thought I'd get to skip altogether arrived? Given how perfectly balanced and poised Tegan has grown up to be, I felt in the clear. But I shouldn't have counted my chickens before they hatched.

"What happened?" I ask.

"The matter and its consequences would be better discussed in person, Miss Hessington. Could you come to pick up your daughter?"

I check my calendar for today. I have another appointment just after lunch, and I can't make it to the Upper West Side and back in time. Thankfully, it's not a hearing. I can reschedule and be at Tegan's school in… "I'll be there in half an hour," I say to Mr. Wentworth.

"Very good, Miss Hessington. I'll see you then."

***

At Tegan's school, the same institute I attended, the walk to reach the principal's office puts me on edge, even if long gone are the days since I was a student here. Still, the halls of TAG High—short for "talented and gifted"—have remained eerily unchanged, with the same dark-red lockers and white tiled floors. The hall becomes darker as I approach Mr. Wentworth's office. A deliberate choice probably set in place to intimidate wrongdoers—or the poor parents who've come to collect them, and who will surely be lectured on their lack of parenting skills.

I turn the last corner of this ominous journey and find Tegan seated on one of the gray plastic chairs lining the wall, waiting alone. Her head is bowed low, and when I stop next to her, she doesn't meet my eyes.

I stomp my boot loudly to get her attention, and she jerks her head up. "What did you do?" I hiss.

Before Tegan can answer, Mrs. Lewis, the Head of School's secretary, hurries out of her cubicle to greet me. "Miss Hessington." She's a chubby woman in her late fifties with gray hair collected at the nape of her neck in a low chignon and dressed in a dark green granny dress. Her only stylish note is the black-rimmed, cat-eye glasses perched on her nose. Underneath the lenses, her gaze is shifty and she's visibly embarrassed. "The principal is waiting for you." Mrs. Lewis addresses Tegan next, "You should both get in."

Like the rest of the school, Mr. Wentworth's office is straight out of a time capsule. Same dark wood décor, books-filled shelves, metal cabinets, and, yep, same old coffee stain on the carpet in the lower-left corner of the principal's desk.

I sit in the empty chair on the left while Tegan sits on the right, the big desk the only thing separating us from the principal's disapproving stare. If I had to describe Mr. Wentworth, I'd say: bald, thin, severe, and with impeccable taste for stuffy tweed suits that belong in the previous century.

"Good morning, Miss Hessington," the principal says. "Sorry we had to rush you here, but the circumstances are quite dire."

I brace myself for whatever is coming next, and the bad news arrives pronto.

"Your daughter, along with several of her peers, was caught consuming alcohol on the school's premises—vodka, to be precise. This not only goes against TAG's policies, but, as I'm sure you're well aware, underage drinking also constitutes a crime."

I turn an incredulous stare on Tegan, but she's too busy staring at her feet to notice.

"Now, if it were only a matter of consumption," the principal continues, "we could let your daughter off with a simple suspension. But since Tegan instigated the drinking and procured the vodka, I'm afraid we have no other choice other than to expel—"

"Wait," I interrupt. "How do you know the alcohol belongs to Tegan?"

I can picture my daughter getting roped into a wrongdoing because of peer pressure—but bringing a bottle of vodka to school and being the instigator of a lunch-break booze fest? Nuh-uh. Not my daughter. Where would she even get the vodka in the first place? I don't keep alcohol at home—not even wine.

"A few of the students involved in the... ah... mischief, indicated your daughter as the one responsible for smuggling the bottle into the school."

I might want to strangle Tegan for how reckless she's been, but my role right now is to do everything in my power not to have her expelled and her life ruined by a stupid mistake. And that's when the lawyer in me takes over.

"Other than this testimony, do you have definitive proof my daughter brought the vodka to school?"

"As I said, a few witnesses have stated—"

I begin my cross-examination.

"How many students were caught drinking?"

"Six. Three boys and three girls, including Tegan."

"And all five of these students claimed Tegan provided the alcohol?"

The principal shifts in his chair, clearly uncomfortable. I imagine he's used to parents being intimidated when he charges their children with wrong-doings. But my attorney-at-law persona is formidable, and the tables have turned on poor Mr. Wentworth. He's no idea what's about to get to him.

"No," he admits. "The boys refused to name any names. But the two girls clearly stated in separate interviews that your daughter—"

"And were the suspects kept apart at all times before these interrogations?"

"No, of course not, we don't have the facilities for—"

"So it's possible they agreed beforehand to blame my daughter?"

"Yes, but—"

"Have you asked Tegan if she's responsible for bringing alcohol to school?"

"Yes, and Tegan has denied it. But she's also refused to reveal the culprit, which is highly suspicious."

I stare at my daughter now. She looks mortified, but her lips are locked in a tight, stubborn line that tells me she's not going to rat out her friends to get off the hook. Not the smartest decision, but I'm aware of how complex high school social hierarchy can be. And since *boys* are involved... I remember what it was to be fifteen and have a crush—the stupid things one could do to impress *a boy*.

Even if Tegan is not willing to help herself, she's lucky she has me as her last line of defense.

"Are the three boys involved facing expulsion as well?"

"No, they weren't named as the culprits."

"But they also refused to provide a name, same as my

daughter. And are these two girls accusing Tegan friends, by any chance?"

"I can't presume to know the relationships linking each student in this school."

I give him a flat look. "You're telling me it's impossible to determine whether or not those two girls are friends? Just ask the teachers, the canteen staff, and their peers, it should be a simple enough connection to investigate."

I stare at Tegan again, forcing her to look up at me for the first time since I arrived with the intensity of my gaze. Reddened blue-gray eyes huge with fear meet mine. "Are these two girls friends?" I ask her directly.

Tegan gives me the smallest nod, but it's enough.

"There you have it," I say to the principal. "Mr. Wentworth, their testimony must be disregarded. It's unreliable at best, and I'd go as far as saying intentionally fraudulent in the worst case. Both witnesses were caught red-handed, are renowned cohorts, and had a pretty obvious motive to make a scapegoat out of my daughter. Other than their word, do you have any other evidence Tegan introduced the alcohol at school?"

Mr. Wentworth's lips are tight. "No."

"Do you have any evidence as to where Tegan acquired the alcohol? Because I assure you I don't keep any spirits in my house. And as you've pointed out, she's underage and can't just walk into a liquor store and buy some."

"She could have a fake ID. You've no idea the things our children can hide from us, Miss Hessington."

Oh, I'm becoming a quick study on the matter.

"Can I see the bottle in question?"

"Why?"

"I would like to examine it."

"What difference does it make?"

"Please humor me."

Visibly rattled, the Head of School pushes an intercom button and asks his secretary to bring in the corpus delicti.

A few tense heartbeats pass in silence before Mrs. Lewis comes into the office and deposits a bottle covered in Swarovski crystals in the center of the desk.

Any lingering doubts that Tegan really did instigate all this mayhem immediately fade from my mind. "Mr. Wentworth, I don't know how familiar you are with expensive liquors, but that right there is a thousand-dollar bottle of vodka. My daughter doesn't have the means to procure such a fine spirit, fake ID or not. If you want to find a culprit, I suggest you look at the size of the trust funds of the other pupils involved."

Mr. Wentworth seems at a loss for words, so I seize the opportunity to ensure Tegan's continued enrollment at this school. "Given what we have discussed, I'm sure we can both agree Tegan should receive an equal punishment to the other students implicated and be charged with a simple suspension."

"Very well." The principal's lips have become even thinner. "Tegan will be charged with a three-day suspension which, provided no other incidents occur, will not be reported on her record. Your daughter will still be expected to complete all her coursework in these three days and turn in her homework on time. The suspension will carry over the weekend, and she also won't be able to play in Saturday's volleyball game against Billard."

Tegan's head snaps up; she's about to protest, but I

silence her with a stare of death. Missing a game will be a severe lesson and a harsher punishment than anything I may come up with.

Mr. Wentworth keeps speaking, "Also, for the following two weeks, all six students must attend an hour-long mandatory detention before first period."

Ah, my share of the sentence for being a terrible mom has arrived. I see my already sleep-deprived self lose even more rest. If Tegan has to be up an hour early, so do I. Unless I want Mr. Wentworth dragging me in here again because of her tardiness.

The Head of School concludes his reprimand with a condescending, "And I suggest you spend some time explaining to your daughter the pitfalls of underage drinking."

With that last jab at my poor parenting skills, Tegan and I are excused.

I march my daughter out of the school, seething with suppressed rage. It takes a full block of speed-walking before I can form coherent speech again. "You're grounded, indefinitely. Drinking vodka at school! How could you be so irresponsible, after all the hard work you've put into having perfect grades? You're lucky this won't affect your permanent record, or you would've just blown up your entire life, and for what? To impress some a rich kid?"

"Mom, I didn't even drink that much! It was only a sip."

I stop walking and turn on her. "Are you really this naïve? Drinking alcohol at your age is illegal, Tegan, even if it's just a sip! And *especially* if you do it on school grounds! Why would you do such a thing? Risk your entire future, and for what? You're not touching another drop of alcohol until you turn twenty-one, do you hear me?"

Tegan scoffs, the demure child gone to be replaced by the surly teenager. "As if you can talk."

"What does that mean? I've never had a problem with alcohol."

"Oh, I'm sorry, you're right," Tegan says sarcastically. "So I should steer clear of the booze, but getting myself pregnant and dumped at nineteen is totally fine?"

That's a low blow. I know it, she knows it, but she's also not backing down at this point. I take a few deep breaths to steady my nerves before I give in to the urge to slap my daughter for the first time in fifteen years. The temptation is strong right now.

Instead, I outstretch my hand. "Your phone. Hand it over."

Reluctantly, she does, smacking it in my open palm.

"I will hold on to this, *also indefinitely*. I'm shutting down the Wi-Fi at home, and from now on you can use your laptop only to do homework. Be this disrespectful again and you're off the volleyball team for good, no matter if it's great for your college resume." Her eyes widen with fear and perceived injustice, but I'm on a roll. "And if I smell another drop of alcohol on you ever again, I'll have you packed and shipped off to a military school for girls only."

Tegan doesn't make any attempt to apologize, but her eyes do widen with dread at my threat. And for now, that will do.

Ten

Lucas

At midday, on Wednesday, I wrap up the last session of the morning, type in a few notes, and then I'm ready to stretch my legs and go out for lunch.

As I walk down the block, I'm surprised to find Medusa's daughter sitting on a bench with a forlorn expression as she stares right ahead.

I stop next to her, asking, "Another half-day?"

Tegan looks up and shakes her head. "No, I've been suspended."

Suspended? This girl seems so self-possessed; she didn't give me the impression of being the suspension type.

I sit next to her. "What happened?"

"Does being a therapist work the same as being a lawyer?"

"I'm not sure... How do you mean?"

"That if I give you, say, a dollar, you're hired and everything I tell you is bound by confidentiality."

I raise my hands defensively. "I can't be your therapist."

"Why not?"

"I have no experience in child counseling."

"Good." Tegan's mouth sets in that same stubborn pout I've witnessed so many times on her mother's face. "Because I'm not a child. On your plaque, it says you're a family specialist."

"Yes, but I've specialized in couples' counseling. And you're a minor, which means I can't provide mental health services without seeking your mother's approval." I scoff. "And I guarantee you I wouldn't be her first choice for a therapist. Or even her last choice, for that matter."

"But I like you. And I don't want to go talk to a total stranger, who'd probably just agree with Mom to keep the checks coming."

"I'm flattered, but I still can't do it. What I can do is recommend a colleague with unquestionable ethics, who will listen to you and not take anyone's side."

"I don't need some stranger telling me what to do."

"That's not what therapists do, Tegan. We don't give orders—we listen, and then we guide patients so they can consciously decide on their own."

Tegan considers this, then sighs. "Never mind. Mom would never pay for therapy anyway; she thinks shrinks are charlatans."

Why doesn't that surprise me? I'm not fresh on the code, but if a minor is seeking a mental health consultation and the legal guardian refuses to provide them access, I could in theory offer my services.

A gray area at best. Still, I've never refused to help someone who sought my counsel, and I'm not starting today.

"Give me that dollar," I say.

Tegan beams at me, pulls a bill out of her jeans pocket, and hands it over.

"Let's go back to my office," I say. "How long before you're supposed to meet with your mother?"

"At least another half an hour, but she's probably going to be late like always."

"All right, chop, chop, then."

***

Back in my office, I'm sitting in my armchair, notepad in hand, while Tegan is the sole occupant of the couch usually reserved for couples.

"Let's start at the beginning," I say. "Why did you get suspended?"

"For drinking vodka at school."

Okay, didn't see that one coming.

"Is drinking alcohol a habit, or was it the first time?"

Tegan shifts in her chair, not answering.

"We're in session," I remind her. "I won't tell your mother anything you say here. Doctor-patient confidentiality."

She blushes. "It wasn't the first time, but I'm not an alcoholic or anything. Sometimes I drink a beer or two at house parties or, you know, stuff like that."

"And I assume your mother has no idea?"

Tegan shakes her head.

And, I have to be honest with myself here, the next question is one hundred percent professionally needed, but I'm not going to pretend it won't satisfy a great curiosity I've had since learning my office neighbor had a daughter.

"What about your father? Does he know?"

Tegan becomes uncomfortable again. "I don't know who my father is."

And I've stumbled on a minefield. From now on, I must tread carefully.

"Does your mother not know, or—"

"Oh, no, she does. She's just refused to tell me point-blank every time I've asked, so I've stopped."

"Has she given you a reason why she doesn't want you to know?"

"Yeah, she said my father wanted nothing to do with me or her after he discovered she was pregnant, and that I'm better off without that bastard in my life."

"And what do you think about that?"

She fidgets with the silver band on her middle finger. "I'd still like to meet him. Even if he chose not to be in my life, I want to know who he is, what he does, if we have anything in common. Half of my genes are his, and I have no clue who the guy is. He could be a stoner loser, or a genius."

"Would it make any difference if he was one or the other?"

"Probably not, but I'd still like to know where I come from. And…" Tegan places both her hands under her thighs on the couch.

"Go ahead," I prompt. "You're safe here, please talk freely."

"I want to ask him why he abandoned me. Mom already has her answer, but I never got mine."

"That's an excellent point, Tegan, and we can work on convincing your mother to reveal your father's name. Or better, even. If you decide therapy is something you want to continue, you and your mother could see a family specialist together. One that would make your mother comfortable, and where she'd feel on neutral ground. I'd love to help you, but I'm not the right person to consult you both."

"Mom would never agree to that."

I really don't want to say this next part, but my personal preferences are outweighed by my professional obligation to help this young woman. "I can talk to her," I offer. "I can try to persuade her to consider a family counseling session. And if that doesn't work, you should ask for help from your school counselor. If the suggestion of therapy came directly from the school, she'd be compelled to listen."

"Would you really talk to her?"

"Yes."

Tegan's face brightens up in a huge smile. "You're the best."

"Easy," I say. "I haven't convinced her yet. And you still haven't told me why you were drinking vodka at school."

The smile disappears, and Tegan removes her hands from under her thighs only to wring them together in her lap. "Well… there's this boy…"

Of course there's a boy involved… I am *talking to a teenage girl.*

"You like him?" I ask.

A shy nod.

"Is this boy your boyfriend, or…?"

"No, gosh, no, nothing like that. But he just broke up with Celia Buchanan a month ago, and I've liked him forever, and I thought he didn't even know I existed. But then yesterday, I went to eat my lunch in the chemistry lab—I do that sometimes when the canteen feels too crowded and I want a bit of quiet. Anyway, Josh was already there with two of his friends. And one of them—Derek—is dating Mykenna Flanagan, so she was there, too, and she doesn't go anywhere without her sidekick Sydney."

"Okay," I say, trying to wrap my head around the complex teenage society.

"They were already drinking when I got there; Josh had stolen a bottle from his father's cabinet, and he invited me to join."

"And you agreed?"

"Yes."

"Why?"

"It would've been super uncool to say no, so lame. And I know what you're thinking…"

"Really? What am I thinking?"

"That it was stupid. That I shouldn't have drunk just to impress a boy or anyone. You're probably going to tell me that I should give up on Josh, because a guy who drinks stolen vodka in the middle of the school day isn't boyfriend material."

"It's not my job to tell you who to date," I say carefully. "But I agree that you should never do something you don't want to do in order to impress someone. But clearly you knew that already, so why did you still agree to drink the vodka?"

"Because I have to go to that school for the next two years, and Mykenna is such a viper. Who knows what rumors she would've spread if I'd said no? It was easier to take a sip, no harm done. It's not like I was drunk."

"And what would have happened if the next thing they offered you was drugs? Would you have said yes, just because it was easier?"

"It's not the same."

"Isn't it?"

Tegan looks away. Point made, message received.

"Is this going on your permanent record?" I ask, wondering just how deep in trouble she is.

"Mr. Wentworth says it won't, as long as I don't get into any more trouble. Mom made sure of that. She saved my ass; Mykenna tried to blame the whole thing on me. If Mom hadn't intervened, I could've been expelled."

I can picture Miss Hessington, Esquire, as a lioness defending her cub with everything she's got.

"And other than keeping you in school, how did your mother react to the situation?"

"She yelled at me, said I'm grounded indefinitely, and confiscated my phone and laptop, so now I'm stuck with this." Tegan opens the lower pocket of her backpack and takes out a relic from the early 2000s, waving the ancient flip phone at me. "No internet, no photos, not even a color screen. Only texts and calls, so she can get ahold of me at all times. And she's promised that if she ever smells alcohol on me again, she's going to ship me off to a military school for girls only."

"And what do you think of that reaction? Was it fair?"

She shrugs. "I guess."

"Did you tell her that?"

Tegan lowers her gaze. "No, I yelled back at her. Hurtful stuff."

"Do you mind me asking what?"

"I told her I'd steer clear of the booze if that was all she cared about, and maybe instead I'd get pregnant and dumped at nineteen like her."

And something I'd thought impossible happens: I feel utter and complete empathy for Medusa. My heart goes out to Vivian. Having her daughter throw her mistakes back in her face in a fit of spite must've been hard.

"Are you proud of that response?"

Tegan shakes her head.

"Have you apologized?"

"No, but I should."

I close my notepad. "Yeah, I agree. A heartfelt apology

will get a huge weight off your chest, and you'll feel much better. Ultimately, your mother was right to be upset about what you did. She probably shouldn't have yelled or threatened you with military school, but you have to remember one thing, Tegan."

"What?"

"Your mom is only human. She's going to make mistakes, just like you and me and the rest of the world. It can't have been easy for her to raise you alone at such a young age, and parents tend to project their kids' failures as their own, making their reaction exaggerated. We're always the hardest with ourselves. But what you did was wrong, and you've admitted as much yourself, so now, you have to accept the consequences. I'll talk to your mother about revealing who your father is, but in the meantime, I'd like to keep working with you on how not to succumb to peer pressure, and how to become more assertive without completely ruining your social life. Does that sound good?"

"Yes, it does."

"Great. So, your homework is to apologize to your mother, and I'll talk to her first thing tomorrow morning. I'd do it today, but I have to go downtown for a conference."

I check my watch, and it looks like I'll have to skip lunch to get there on time. And that's not even the worst part, as I sure don't look forward to having the you-should-tell-your-daughter-who-her-father-is conversation with Medusa.

Eleven

Vivian

When I meet Tegan for lunch outside my office building, I can immediately tell something is different. The scowl she's dutifully worn since yesterday has been replaced by a tentatively open expression. And, if not completely welcoming, at least she doesn't look like she's about to bite my head off.

Not an ideal state of things, but I'll take it. Anything is better than yesterday's attitude. To further confirm that a mood shift has taken place, when I ask Tegan where she wants to have lunch, she doesn't give me a cheeky or sarcastic answer like "Wherever war prisoners may eat," or "I'd like a homemade meal prepared by my mom's loving hands for a change."

Tegan just shrugs and says, "How about tacos?"

I smile, despite my resolution of keeping a stern, severe, you-really-screwed-up-this-time-kiddo attitude for the entire duration of her suspension, and say, "Tacos sound wonderful."

We go to our favorite taqueria in Brooklyn, and once the meal is over, the second surprise of the day arrives.

Tegan polishes the last crumbs of her tortilla from her plate, takes a sip of Coke, and then looks up at me, sighing a heavy, "Mom?"

"Yes?" I say, bracing myself for whatever will come next. Is she going to ask me for her phone back, or to let her go to the game on Saturday? I must stay strong and refuse all attempts at buttering me up. Vodka Gate could've ruined her chances to get accepted to a good college. And if she can't see how serious the topic is, I need to be the responsible adult and show her that choices have consequences. Even if it sucks just as much for me to enforce the rules as it does for her to follow them.

"I wanted to apologize for yesterday."

"For which part?" I say dryly.

She looks down at her interlaced hands in her lap. "All of it. I'm sorry for drinking at school; I know it was stupid... But I'm also sorry for what I said afterward, to you."

A little string pulls in my chest. For as much as Tegan's words were hurtful yesterday, her apology today is heartwarming. Damn, she's good. If she wanted to find a perfect way to stroke my mommy feathers, she just did. I inwardly prep myself for the upcoming ask. "And?"

"And nothing. I was mad at myself because I'd acted foolishly and got caught, and I was mad at those bitches Mykenna and Sydney because they tried to pin it all on me when it wasn't my fault, and I took it out on you. I was mean, and I'm sorry. Whatever punishment I get, I deserved it. And, Mom, I know you've made a lot of sacrifices to raise me on your own, and you've always been in my corner. You didn't deserve for me to lash out the way I did yesterday. I'm sorry."

Okay, whatever Tegan asks next, she can have. No mom's heart could resist such a declaration. I'm barely able to contain the tears, and I'm even willing to slide past her calling her classmates names. Those two sure sounded like bitches.

I reach across the table to hold Tegan's hand, and the fact

that she lets me is already a sign of how momentous the circumstance is. "Thank you," I whisper.

Tegan nods and, to my utter astonishment, doesn't ask for anything in return. No phone, no volleyball game, no laptop. Yesterday, she made me question my ability to be a good mother by her reckless behavior; and now, today, she goes and behaves like this perfect human.

It is true kids never cease to amaze.

***

That night, at home, I decide to investigate the vodka incident a little deeper. It's easier to look at the facts now that my anger has subsided and logic can take over. I need to understand what drove my rule-following, perfectionist of a daughter to such an act of rebellion. And given the rare moment of confidence we shared at lunch, I'm pretty sure I can get her to talk if I ask the right questions.

Once dinner is over, I take a carton of ice cream out of the fridge—the heavy stuff—and grab two spoons. Nothing says mother-daughter bonding like cookie dough.

I offer a spoon to Tegan and sit next to her so we're sharing a corner of the table.

"Honey, would you mind if I asked you a few questions about what happened at school?"

She shrugs without replying. At least it's not a hard "no" which, when dealing with a teen, I've painfully learned it should already be counted as a victory.

"Have those girls been mean to you in the past? Are they bullying you?"

"No, Mom, don't worry, Mykenna Flanagan and I never hang in the same circles. I was in the wrong place at the wrong time, that's all."

"Why did you drink, then? If you don't care about what this Mykenna thinks... Was it because of a boy? You like one of them?"

"Mom!" Tegan drops her spoon and blushes tomato red. "You can't ask me that!"

"Why not? There's nothing wrong with liking someone... although maybe I wouldn't have picked a boy who brings alcohol to school... And you don't want to date a spoiled rich kid; trust me, they're the worst."

"That's exactly why we can't talk about boys. You're too prejudiced about men."

"I'm not."

"Yes, you are. You only fall for the improbable characters of romance movies. When have you ever given a chance to a real man, like, in real life?"

Stung by her words, even if they're a little more accurate than I'm willing to admit, I say, "Well, Tegan, good men are hard to come by. And I do take chances with men."

"Give me one example," she challenges.

Thank goodness I let Lee persuade me into joining that dating service; otherwise, I'd be eating my own words right now. "I've joined a dating agency," I announce, and Tegan's jaw drops. "The same one Lee used to meet Garrett. Is that enough *out there* for you?"

"Really, Mom?" Tegan throws her arms around my neck, side-hugging me from her chair. "I'm so happy for you! I'm sure you're going to find someone. I can't wait to meet him."

She lets go, and I study her bright smile, perplexed. I hadn't been sure what to expect when I told her, but such boundless enthusiasm hadn't even crossed my mind as a possibility. I have to admit, it feels nice to have my daughter's whole-hearted support—especially after the blow-up we had yesterday. Tegan's the most important person in the world to me, and I hate it when we're at odds.

I hug her back, smoothing down her hair, then push away with a smile. "Easy, tiger," I say. "I've just started the process, and there are no guarantees it's going to work."

"If it worked for Lee and Garrett, why shouldn't it work for you?"

"Good point, let's stay optimistic. And nice try, but I haven't forgotten we were talking about you, not me."

Tegan grins, a bit sheepishly. "Can't blame a girl for trying."

I laugh. "I guess not. Honey... It's hard to talk about this kind of stuff. I get that. But if you don't want to tell me exactly what happened at school, you still need to discuss it with someone. How about Mrs. Simmons? You've always liked your school counselor."

"Don't worry, Mom, I've already talked to someone."

"I meant an adult; your friends don't count."

"He is an adult."

I frown. "He? Who's 'he'?"

Tegan lowers her gaze, and I brace myself for another horrible revelation. Did a perv on the internet string her along? I don't even know what I'm dreading to hear when she says, "My therapist."

At first I'm relieved. Then my thoughts start to whirl. Where on Earth did she find a therapist on such short notice? Or has she been seeing him for a while? And how is she paying for this therapy? Has she been giving all her savings to someone who spouts comforting nonsense and creates problems where none exist? How much? A professional can't be cheap. Where did she get the money?

I want to fire all these questions and concerns at her, but I sense I'd better tread carefully. We've reached a fragile balance where she's talking to me again and giving me a peek into her secretive teen life; I don't want to spook her into closing all communication channels. And even if I'm not a fan of shrinks, I suppose it's still a positive sign that Tegan reached out to one... especially considering this brand-new, law-breaking side of her I had no idea existed.

"A therapist," I repeat, making my voice as calm and untroubled as possible. "I see. What's his name? Is he part of some free counseling program offered by the city or the school? Or am I going to panic when I see my next credit card bill?"

Tegan lowers her gaze again, making my heart jump in my throat. Oh gosh, why the guilty expression? What's about to hit me this time?

Tegan looks up with a curious set to her jaw, like she's steeling herself to say something. "No, Mom, he isn't part of a special program. He's just a normal therapist that you hire. And he's kind of doing it pro-bono."

I narrow my eyes at her. "Who's *he,* exactly?"

"Luke. That nice man with the office next to yours?"

My brain takes a few extra seconds to figure out who she's talking about, because *nice man* doesn't fit my mental characterization of the ogre next door.

Oh, burning hell, no! Of all the people Tegan could talk to, she went to Shrek? *Shrink Shrek?* And how dare he talk to my daughter without asking for my permission? I'm going to have his license revoked faster than he can—

"And Mom, before you go ballistic—Luke is a wonderful therapist."

I scoff in my head, so I keep hearing.

"He helped me see things from a different perspective…"

"Really, which prospective?"

"*Yours.*"

I pause, momentarily thrown. "Is that why you apologized to me today? Because he told you to?"

"No, Mom, he didn't *tell* me. Luke made me see it was the right thing to do."

Tegan's answer is so annoyingly perfect and impossible to retort to, it makes me want to strangle someone. A very specific blue-eyed, curly-dark-haired someone.

Twelve

Lucas

Early on Thursday morning, a loud, angry pounding on my office door distracts me from the computer. I don't have any sessions planned for at least another hour, so it's probably not one of my patients. When the banging continues, I get up from my chair and warily approach the door.

The moment I open it, Medusa barks in my face, "I'm going to have your license revoked!"

Medusa is so worked up, even her bun isn't as composed as usual. Instead of the sleek curtain of hair glued to her scalp, haywire locks are escaping in all directions. The new hairstyle makes her look more human, even, dare I say, cute. Pity that it's framing a face so enraged it has lost all cuteness.

"According to New York MHY 33.21," she rails at me, "in providing outpatient mental health services to a minor, the important role of the parents or guardians shall be recognized. That's *me*." She jabs her thumb against her chest for emphasis.

I know I should keep calm and be reasonable, seeing as this is a professional matter, but this woman has the extraordinary power of pushing all my buttons quicker than an arcade champion playing Space Invaders. How dare she storm in here and threaten my career when I was just trying to help?

"Instead of worrying about having my license revoked," I retort, "you should ask yourself why your daughter came to seek my help. And while you're at it, have a good look in the mirror."

Outrage marks her features now. "You have *no* idea the amount of trouble you'll find yourself in if you don't stop meddling in my daughter's affairs."

"Well, *someone* has to deal with her problems, since you clearly don't! All Tegan needs is for someone to listen to her."

Indignation turns to hurt, then switches quickly back to fury. Without another word, Medusa pivots on her heel, stomps off into her office, and slams the door shut. I follow her example and slam my own door equally loudly.

And now I feel like shit.

I swear that woman brings out the worst in me. She makes me so infuriated, I completely forget myself. Just now, I wasn't dealing with the obnoxious witch who stole my corner office. I was talking to a patient's parent, which required me to be calm, professional, and understanding. And I was none of those things. But worst of all, I wasn't fair, not on any level—human or professional. I owe Medusa an apology and Tegan a real shot at perorating her cause.

So, no matter how much it sucks, I pick up the proverbial hat in my hands, grab my keys, and reopen the door I so-dramatically slammed shut not a minute ago.

In the landing, a pretty redhead in a light-blue dress and beaded sandals is being escorted into the offices of Inceptor Magazine by that nice Indian woman who welcomed me into the building on move-in day—Indira, I think her name was? Next to each other, the two women make for an odd couple. The redhead looks like she just glided off a catwalk in Milan, while Indira is in her usual all-dark grunge clothes and Converse sneakers. Their attitudes are as different as their outfits. Indira is sporting a cocksure grin, while the redhead looks like someone who just entered a madhouse and isn't sure why. I hope they didn't overhear my unprofessional exchange with Medusa.

The metal and glass doors of the startup close behind them, and I have no more excuses left to put off the inevitable.

I walk to Medusa's door, take a steadying breath, and knock.

Miss Attorney comes to answer right away, and when she finds me on her doorstep, her eyes narrow.

"What do you want?" she says coldly. "Come to dispense some more of your cheap psychology?"

Steady, Luke, keep calm. Don't fall into the trap a second time. She's your patient's caregiver. Treat her like you would any other parent.

I take another long, pacifying inhale before I speak. "I'm here to apologize." Medusa's eyes go wide, like she's too stunned by my declaration to retort, so I say my piece in one breath before she can cut me off. "Earlier, you attacked me, and, given our history of dysfunctional interactions, I behaved unprofessionally, and, frankly, just plain rudely. I was wrong, and what I said wasn't fair, on any level. I had no right to critique your parenting or imply in any way that you aren't an excellent mother. For that, I'm deeply sorry, and I apologize."

Medusa is clearly flabbergasted, but her feisty personality quickly shines through the stupor. She crosses her arms over her chest and regards me with a satisfied pout.

"That said," I continue, "Tegan came to me seeking help. Your daughter told me she needed someone to talk to and that you're averse to psychoanalysis and would've never let her see a professional—"

"That's not true," Medusa interrupts. "I encouraged her to seek the support of her school counselor, who is nice and trustworthy. Contrary to you."

I raise my hands in a not-so-quick gesture. "Tegan felt you wouldn't have supported her if she told you about the matter she really wanted to discuss."

"Which is? Does she have other problems besides vodka-fueled lunch breaks?"

"Yes."

"Like what?"

"Like the mystery father whose identity you refuse to reveal." Medusa's jaw drops, but I continue, undeterred. "She has allowed me to share some details of our conversation with you. We should schedule a session to examine the issue in a more peaceful context than our landing after an altercation." I take a business card out of my suit jacket and offer it to her. "Call me whenever you feel ready to discuss the matter in a civilized way."

The expression of satisfaction adorning her face after my apology has been wiped out, and her coloring is veering toward a shade of red brighter than the soles of her Louboutins.

I take that as my clue to leave now, before her fuse blows. "Given the peculiar circumstances, I won't be charging you any fee," I conclude. "I wish you a nice day."

Her eyes blaze with suppressed anger, and in my head her haywire locks of hair have turned to actual snakes hissing at me for how enraged she looks. It seems my offer to provide free mental health care has sent Medusa off the cliff of her patience, so with a polite goodbye nod, I escape to the safety of my office.

Once inside, I rest my back on the door, closing my eyes and tilting my head up toward the ceiling. I'm already sporting the first symptoms of an incoming headache. If I could go back in time, I'd agree to pay my old landlord double rent, just so I wouldn't have had to move here. This place is causing me more stress than financial instability ever could.

The thought has barely left my brain when an incessant pounding makes the door behind me tremble.

I swear, if she's looking for *another* apology…

"First off, I don't need anyone's charity," Medusa declares, the moment I open the door. "Second, you're going to tell me everything Tegan said about her father, and not just *some details of your conversation she's allowed you to share*, or I'll sue your ass faster than you can say 'malpractice.' And you can take *this* back"—she gives me a candy-coated-poison smirk and tucks my business card back into my pocket, then pats my chest—"and stick it up your… Well, use your imagination. And a nice day to you, too. Come see me whenever *you* are ready to discuss the matter in a civilized way."

Medusa turns on her heel once again and sashays back to her office. I let her go. I've had enough of that infernal woman for one day.

The moment I close the door, I pinch my nose to prevent the headache from spreading and count to ten to calm down. When I reach seven, another knock, this time gentler, makes me jump.

What now? I was just trying to help someone, universe,

why am I being punished?

I open the door. "Something you forgot?"

Medusa is standing on the other side, her expression strangely contrite. "My keys, actually. I've locked myself out."

Ah.

I cross my arms over my chest and lean against the doorframe. "And? I don't have them."

"I was wondering if I might climb out your window and use the fire escape to get into my office." Her face contorts in a weird grimace, which I'm sure she's trying to pass off as an endearing smile.

"Can't you call Leslie, or the building manager? They must have a spare key."

"That would take too long; I have to be in court in an hour, and my briefcase with my pass and all my notes is locked inside."

"All right," I say. "You can come in, on one condition."

"What?"

"Say 'please.'"

I watch the battle between pride and necessity take place on her face, until, finally, with a theatrical roll of her eyes, she mumbles, "Please."

I tap my ear. "Sorry, I couldn't hear that."

Medusa looks me straight in the eye and, gosh, if she doesn't have the most beautiful, big, angry eyes. "I said, *please.*"

I move aside and gesture to my office. "Come on in."

And if witches, like vampires, require an invitation to walk into someone's house, I've just screwed my chances of ever being at peace.

Not one to waste time, Medusa walks briskly across my office to reach the side window overlooking the fire escape. She pulls up the sash, and then pauses, staring at the open window. It takes me a moment to realize why, and I can't help but chuckle.

"Wait here," I tell her, walking over. "I'll go."

"There's no need. I'm perfectly capable of going myself."

I give her a pointed once-over, taking in her stilettos and impossibly tight pencil skirt. "In that skirt and those shoes? Be my guest, if you can climb out of the window, you can go."

She steps next to the window across from me and awkwardly tries to raise a leg over the windowsill, failing. Medusa pauses to debate her alternatives. I can practically see the gears in her head turning. She can either raise her skirt above her thighs and go outside, I'm not complaining, or admit she's wrong and let me do the job. To be honest, I'm not sure which alternative *I*'d prefer.

Finally, with a frustrated huff, she waves a hand at me. "Okay, you go."

I remove my jacket, drop it on the patients' couch, and climb out to the fire escape. A short walk across the black metal platform brings me to her office window. It's closed.

"Your window's locked," I call back.

Medusa pokes her head out, surveying the situation. Then, after nibbling briefly at her pinky, she says. "That one is, but the one next to it is open."

The "one next to it" is a good six feet from the edge of the fire escape.

"Are you crazy?" I demand. "You want me to climb outside the ramp?"

"No, *I* want to climb outside the ramp. Nobody asked you to intervene. If you have a pair of sweatpants I can borrow, I'll do it myself. It's barely a three-foot walk on the ledge."

"Three stories above ground!" I protest.

She just looks at me. "Please?"

With a few angry yanks, I remove my shoes and socks and throw them onto the fire escape. If I have to play Spider-Man, leather Italian shoes are not the way to go.

Shaking my head all along, I climb over the railing. One leg first, then the other. As I swing the second leg over the bar, my trousers catch on a piece of protruding metal. I hear the distinctive noise of fabric tearing as my left foot is about to land on the wrong side of the railing. The sound distracts me. I slip, losing my grip on the railing, and begin to fall.

Thirteen

Vivian

I may not have much affection in my heart for Dr. Meddling, but I still shriek in horror as I watch him suddenly plummet off the edge of the fire escape toward certain death.

Luckily the doctor has good reflexes and is able to grab onto the railing's metal bars at the last second thus avoiding a horrible end splattered on the curb below. Shrek ends up dangling from the bottom of this level of the fire escape like a worm on a hook. Not dead, but not too comfortable either.

"Are you okay?" I call.

"Do I look okay to you?"

It's weirdly comforting that, even when facing a horrible death, he hasn't lost the will to fight with me.

"Can you climb back up?" I ask hopefully.

"A hand would be nice. I'm a therapist, not a world champion in parkour!"

I push off the windowsill and stare at my pencil skirt. Well, I'm not climbing out wearing this. I pull down the rear zipper and shimmy out, then I remove my jacket, and kick off my shoes. Freed from my constrictive clothing, I climb easily through the window, grateful that my blouse is long enough to reach below my buttocks—*barely*.

I hurry to the other end of the fire escape, lean my torso out, and offer Shrink Shrek a hand. Lucas grabs it and, holding on to me, he's able to climb up until our eyes are level again. Well, almost level, since Dr. Keller is a few inches taller than me.

Without another word, Shrek uses the handle of the moving fire stair above ours as a handgrip and climbs further until both his feet are on the railing. From this perching position, he turns around and carefully walks along the ledge toward my open window, regaling me a second peek of white boxer briefs underneath torn pants.

Another step, and he's able to crawl inside my office through the open window.

A stingy gush of wind prompts me to rush back into Shrek's office and get dressed. Before I leave, since I have no idea where Lucas keeps his keys, I use one of the blue-cloth psychology tomes covering the shelves of the sidewall to stop the door from locking behind me.

I step on the landing just as Lucas comes out of my office, keeping the door open for me. He doesn't look happy.

I approach him with caution and say, "Thank you."

"You're welcome. Let's never do this again."

"Well, none of it would've happened if you hadn't stuck your nose into my affairs."

He gives me an incredulous, are-you-being-serious-right-now stare. So I backtrack a little. "I'm grateful you helped me with the keys. But I meant what I said: I want you to stay out of my daughter's life."

"It's a pity, then, that I just risked my life to get you to court on time, because now you owe me one. And I'm cashing in right now. You're going to listen to what Tegan has to say about her father, whether you like it or not. Then we'll be square." Before I can protest, he adds, "And I agree I shouldn't be your therapist. But Tegan reached out to me, and I promised her I would talk to you, so that's what we're going to do. Then, I'm going to refer you both to a family specialist. But now's not the time. You have an appointment, and I need to take a shower. I hadn't planned for an impromptu mountain-climbing training session in the middle of my morning. Once again, a nice day to you, and please don't come knocking on my door for at least another week."

With that, he storms across the landing, looking not half bad with his tousled hair, dress-shirt messily hanging out of his pants, rolled-up sleeves, and bare feet. The bossy attitude is kind of hot, too. If Shrek wasn't the horrible man-ogre he is, I could even—

I censor the thought before it can take shape in my head.

Instead, I call after him, "You tore your—"

"I know," he snaps, stopping at his door. "I'm not sure if you're costing me more in emotional damages or sartorial bills."

He picks up the book from the floor and disappears inside his office.

Fourteen

Lucas

On Saturday night, I arrive at the restaurant at eight on the dot. I give the hostess my fake name, and with a bright smile she guides me to my table, saying, "Please follow me, Mr. Ewing, your date is already here."

As we meander through the restaurant's tables, I have to confess I'm nervous. Especially when I spot a woman with strawberry blonde hair sitting alone at a table toward the rear of the room, her back turned to us. I still can't believe I agreed to a blind date. The few times I've tried one of those in the past, before Brenda, they all resulted in fiascos.

But tonight, if nothing else, I'm sure the worst highlight of the week is behind me. I mean, what could be worse than hanging from a fire escape a handgrip away from certain death and with my butt showing? Talk about adding insult to injury. The reminiscence triggers another, even less welcome memory: one of long legs and lacy pink underwear.

The male brain is a weird organ. I was at a concrete risk of dying a very painful death, and I had the time to check out Medusa's unexpectedly racy panties as she came to my rescue. The bright pink lace was kind of hard to ignore, given the unfortunate perspective, but still, my pesky encephalon's priorities are definitely skewed.

Because your brain is not the organ you were thinking with, a nasty little voice says in my head.

Right. And I'd better not brood over a woman's lingerie when I'm about to meet another one for the first time. Now is the moment to concentrate on tonight, and the surely delightful Miss Bishop.

The hostess stops next to the blonde, saying, "This is your table, Mr. Ewing," and then leaves.

The mysterious Miss Bishop turns her face up and our eyes meet for the first time. Hers are a dark blue-green shade, and she is… honestly, a very beautiful woman. Fresh-faced, without too much makeup on, and with an open, friendly expression. And when she beams at me in welcome, two cute dimples appear at the sides of her mouth.

She gets up, saying, "Hi." Then she smiles again and blushes a little, adding, "Sorry, I'm nervous. I'm not used to, you know, all this." She waves at me and the table. "But a friend convinced me I *had* to give *Listen to Your Heart* a try, so here we are. I don't even know how we should greet. A handshake seems too formal, and a hug too forward?"

The blabbered introduction puts me immediately at ease. Miss Bishop is just another human being who has been roped into joining a dating agency by her pushy friends.

"I'm fine with a hug, if you are?"

She nods, and we share the briefest of embarrassed hugs.

I push her chair in for her, then move to the other side of the table, sit down, and place my napkin on my legs.

"All right, Miss Bishop, I believe we're now allowed to share our real names. I'm Lucas—Luke."

"I'm Meadow."

"What a pretty name. I love it."

She blushes again. "Thanks."

"I hope you like the restaurant I picked. The menu is mostly meat, but the agency assured me you're an omnivore."

Meadow chuckles. "This place is perfect, and steak is my favorite. And, oh, gosh, can you believe the list of diets on that questionnaire? I wasn't sure what half of them were."

Okay, Garrett, maybe you had a point, and this dating agency idea isn't so crazy after all.

"I know, right?" I say. "Can I ask you something?"

"Yeah, sure."

"Why did you pick the alias of Bishop? Is it a famous name?"

"Bridget Bishop was the first witch hanged at the Salem trials."

I'm slightly taken aback by the declaration but try to spin it on the positive side. "Oh, are you passionate about history?"

"Yes, it's important to learn who our ancestors were. The Puritan era is such a dark splotch in this country's past. Don't you agree?"

"Absolutely." I try to bring the conversation back onto less loaded topics. "I'm afraid my alias is much less poetic—"

"Come on, don't discount number 33, he's a legend!"

"Are you a Knicks fan?" I ask, surprised, my good mood restored at once.

"Yes," Meadow says. Then she leans in closer with a conspiratorial air. "I have to admit the agency tricked me into going on a date tonight, and they only managed because it's an away game."

I laugh. "Same here."

A server arrives, asking if we're ready to order drinks or if we've chosen our food already.

Meadow looks at me. "I'm having the steak, but if you

106

need more time…"

"No," I say. "I'll have the steak as well."

I take in her warm smile, add in our shared love of basketball and passion for the same foods, and imagine what a future with this woman would look like. A few years of passionate nights spent making love, Knicks games, and wild travels… Then we would settle down, have a couple of kids, and bring them to Madison Square Garden as soon as they were old enough to enjoy a game… It could work. Maybe taking the randomness out of the meeting process is not as unromantic as I originally thought, and the algorithm really knows best.

The server jots down our orders and turns to Meadow. "How would you like your steak done, ma'am?"

"Rare," she says.

"Very well." The server writes her preference and then asks me the same question. "And you, sir?"

"Medium rare, please."

More scribbling. "And to drink?"

I look at Meadow. "Would you like to share a bottle of wine, or is a glass enough?"

She smiles, embarrassed. "A glass might be better; I'm such a lightweight."

We both order a glass of red.

"Perfect," the server says. "I'll be right back with your drinks."

Once we're alone again, Meadow straightens the napkin on her legs, looking shy. "What did you answer to your ideal day question? I mean, if we're even allowed to discuss our questionnaires?"

"I won't tell if you don't."

She smiles, those adorable dimples making another appearance, just as the server arrives with our wine glasses.

I take a sip and then answer her question. "I've always wanted to finish the Stairway to Heaven Trail up in Mountain Creek. Do you enjoy hiking?"

"Yeah, I love being in nature. I went into the woods around Westchester just the other weekend, up the old Buckout Road for the full moon."

"Did you say full moon? As in, you went at night?"

"Yes, the forest has much stronger energy after dusk."

"Isn't it dangerous?"

"Not if you have the right spiritual guide. And there are also less prying eyes."

Did she say *spiritual* guide? What did she mean? I let the comment slide, and ask, "Not a fan of the crowds, uh?"

"Large congregations can be powerful, but when I'm in the woods, Artemis is the only companion I need."

"Err, your dog?" I ask hopefully.

"No, silly." Meadow laughs me off. "The Greek goddess of the moon and female independence."

Err... how do I respond to that? Thankfully, I'm saved the task by the server bringing our food.

He puts down her plate first, then mine, saying, "Let me know if I can do anything else for you. Ma'am, I hope your steak isn't too bloody."

With the sweetest smile, Meadow replies, "Oh, the bloodier the better. We wouldn't want to waste such a powerful conduit."

Alarm bells have been ringing in my brain for a while now, but I ignore yet another reference to the supernatural and try to keep the conversation going.

"How's your steak?"

"Great, yours?"

"Yeah, wonderful."

A small silence follows, and I fill it with the only topic I can think of, reciprocating her earlier question. "What did you put as your ideal day off?"

"Oh, every chance I get, I drive up to Sleepy Hollow."

The alarm bells ring again.

"Mmm, Sleepy Hollow, like the movie? Is that a real place?"

"Yes, it's a small town up north. Can you believe we live in such a big city, but are blessed by having such a mystical place not thirty miles away? Naturally, all the stories about a headless horseman are crap."

"Right," I agree with her, relief washing over me.

"But the village has been touched by magic."

And the anxiety is back. I can't ignore the facts anymore. Meadow picked a long-dead witch as her alias, she likes to hike in the woods alone at night, talks of blood as a powerful conduit, and spends her free time in a folkloric village allegedly *touched by magic.*

I'm not sure how to phrase my next question and opt for the most direct route. "Do you... err... believe in magic?"

Meadow looks me straight in the eyes with that open smile and cute dimples. "Of course I believe in magic. I'm a witch."

My stomach sinks, and no matter how delicious the steak tastes, I suddenly lose all my appetite. Apparently, having a witch as an office neighbor wasn't enough; now, I've also gotten myself on a date with one. A more superstitious man could think he'd been cursed.

After Meadow's casual admission, I have no idea how to move the conversation forward. So, when my phone vibrates in my pocket, I take it out. Normally I wouldn't do this on a date, but... given the circumstances...

"Sorry," I say. "I'm a doctor, and this might be a patient needing my help."

"Don't worry," Meadows says, still busy enjoying her bloody steak.

That's when I realize we didn't even get down to the part of telling each other what our jobs are. I mean, what do witches do for a living? Besides being divorce lawyers, of course.

Speaking of the devil, I check my messages, and see I have a string of incoming texts from Tegan.

> SOS
>
> Mom wants to take me to an AA meeting open to "endangered" teens
>
> Can you get me out of it?

I shake my head as I reply. Medusa sure took the vodka incident to heart.

> No can do, sorry

> And I'm not saying it's
> necessary, but it won't do
> you any harm to go

No harm?

I'll be scarred for life after
this

I can't suppress a smirk; the daughter has a dry sense of humor she hasn't inherited from her mother. And, at the cost of sounding sanctimonious, I reply:

> Wrong deeds have
> consequences

> You must accept them and
> the scars they bring

Then I add a smiley emoji so as not to sound too preachy.

I put the phone away and imagine the two of them, mother and daughter, walking into a grim underground room equipped with free coffee, donuts, and a lot of gloomy feelings. And the sad truth is that, right now, I'd rather be at an AA meeting for "endangered" teens with Tegan and Vivian instead of having to spend another minute on this date. I mean, at least they get free donuts.

Even knowing my acquaintance with Meadow is doomed and will be as short-lived as our dinner, I keep making polite conversation for the rest of the evening. But when the end of the meal finally arrives, I don't know how to say goodbye. The witch and I aren't going on a second date, that's for sure. But how can I break the news gently? Witches deserve to have their feelings spared like any other woman. Assuming Meadow is interested in a second date at all. Should I even say anything, or will the agency take care of everything? Jennifer, my Dating Specialist, said something about a follow-up call to collect feedback.

I take a sip of water, trying to decide how to say goodbye, when Meadow, with the most casual tone in the world, says, "This has been a wonderful evening. Do you want to go have sex?"

Half the water spurts out of my mouth, splattering on myself and my half of the table, but thankfully not reaching Meadow.

I use my napkin to dry my face. "Excuse me?" And just because I can't have heard her right, I say, "You asked me if I wanted to go have sex?"

With the same easygoing attitude, Meadow says, "Yeah, I want to do a scrying ritual at midnight; a friend has asked me to take a peek into her future. And sex is great to raise earthly energy and create magical power."

Sorry, that'll be a hard pass. Also, Garrett, you're so dead.

Fifteen

Vivian

"Who are you texting?" I ask my daughter. "Aren't all your friends on WhatsApp or Snapchat these days? I thought texts were dead."

"I'm not chatting with my friends," Tegan replies, her thumbs moving over the buttons of the ancient phone I gave her for emergencies. Composing a text is taking her thrice the time it'd take on a modern smartphone.

"Who are you texting, then?" I repeat, annoyed she's purposely giving me half-answers.

Tegan puts her thumbs on hold for a second and stares up at me. "My therapist."

Heat floods my cheeks. "That man is not your therapist, and why are you texting him?"

"To ask him if he can get me out of this crazy idea you've gotten into your head. I don't need an AA meeting, Mom."

Her phone pings. Tegan reads the text, and frowns.

"So?"

"Luke says AA isn't necessary."

"Really?" Shrek can be a pain to deal with, but he doesn't strike me as someone who'd so blatantly undermine a parent's authority, especially not when he's wearing his therapist hat. She must be paraphrasing. "Is that all?"

Tegan sighs. "No, he also says it won't do me any harm."

"Now that we have your therapist's blessing, can we go?" We're standing in the tiny entrance hall of our house, already dressed and ready to leave. Only, Tegan has dug her metaphorical heels into the carpet and is refusing to get out.

"Mom, please. I promise I won't drink again until I'm twenty-one, but can we please not go?" And I swear, I've had to deal with my fair share of hard-bitten opposing counsels, but I'm quickly discovering they're all amateurs compared to a teenager who thinks she's being treated unfairly. "I already missed the game today, and all my friends are out having fun. And it's okay that I'm grounded but going to an AA meeting is just lame. I'm not an alcoholic. What if someone recognizes us?"

"The people there don't care who you are, Tegan. That's why it's called Alcoholics *Anonymous*."

"But what if we bump into someone we know? What will they think of us?"

"Same you'd think about them: that they have a problem and are trying to cope with it."

"I don't have a drinking problem! It was just one mistake, Mom. This is stupid."

"You think this is how I wanted to spend my Saturday night?"

"Why? You had something better to do? You never go out."

"For your information, I had a match at the dating agency and was supposed to be on my first date tonight."

"And you didn't go because of this? Why? We could've gone any other day."

"No, the meeting I'm taking you to is specifically tailored for teens. People your age and older will share their stories, and I want you to listen to them carefully, so maybe next time someone offers you a drink at school you'll know how to say no."

"Or, you were scared to go on your first date in forever,

and are using your"—Tegan makes a theatrical expression, moving her arms all over the place—"*deranged* daughter as an excuse."

I stare her down without replying.

After a few long seconds, she lowers her gaze. "Sorry, that wasn't fair."

I nod, just as her phone pings with three incoming messages.

"Your *therapist?*" I ask icily.

Tegan nods.

"What does he have to say now?"

She doesn't answer me, and precedes me out of the house, protesting, "This is bullshit."

"Language, young lady," I call as I follow her. "Unless you want to spend next Saturday at a meeting for disrespectful teens." I lock the door to our brownstone townhouse and prepare myself for a bleak few hours.

How I miss tiny rompers and even diaper changes, to be honest, when my biggest problem was breast or bottle. Those were the real golden years. I should've listened to all the people who told me to enjoy them because *kids grow up so fast things only get worse and wait until they're teenagers.*

Unfortunately, the wait is *so* over.

***

The rest of the weekend passes just as dimly. Sunday, it rains all day, so Tegan and I are stuck in the house with our respective grudges. The only highlight is a call from Leslie mid-afternoon with a funny report about Dr. Ogre and his first agency date. Monday morning, I'm still mentally chuckling about it, when the subject of the call walks into the elevator next to me. Lucas is wearing another one of his sleek, tailored suits, and his leather shoes risk blinding me with how shiny they are. His hair, on the contrary, is as unruly as his clothes are impeccable, and also damp, as if he just got out of the shower after spending the night rumpling the sheets.

I can assume that's not the case, given what I know, but still, it's annoying for him to be this good looking so early on a Monday morning when the rest of us had to struggle to look half presentable.

"Morning," I say with a big smile.

He takes in my greeting, and frowns. "You're smiling. Something must be terribly wrong in the world."

"No, I'm just in a good mood."

Luke pushes the button to our floor warily, and asks, "Why?"

I shrug. "I'm counting the days until you'll have to move out."

"And what gives you such an unfounded certainty?"

"I heard you went on quite a... ah... *magical* date on Saturday."

The scowl deepens, and I watch the creases on his forehead become more pronounced as he does the math: he told Garrett about his date, Garrett told Leslie, and Lee told me.

I expect a dry retort about my own AA Saturday night, but Luke shrugs, saying, "Beginner's bad luck."

I'm so shocked, I have to prod him. "What? No jabs about my own Saturday night's woes? I know Tegan told you how we spent the evening."

"Being a good parent is not something I find tasteful jabbing about."

Lucas' comment shocks me into silence and gives me more pleasure than it should. I shouldn't seek this man's approval. I shouldn't seek *any* man's approval. But, being a single mother, it's so easy to get judged for my shortcomings as a parent and for not always being able to stretch this one person to do a two-person job, that I can't help feeling a little pride.

When I don't speak again, Lucas fills the silence. "What are you doing at the office so early, anyway? You're never in before eight."

"Tracking my movements now?"

"Hard not to when your heels are so loud on the landing and you shut your door with the grace of an elephant."

I bristle, promising myself to slam the door even harder from now on. "Tegan has an hour detention before school every morning for the next two weeks. I thought I'd use the extra hour productively."

Something good has to come out of having to turn back my alarm clock to five-thirty a.m. for two weeks, or I'd go insane. I already hate getting up early Monday through Friday but cutting an extra hour of sleep is pure torture. Another of the many joys of parenting.

"So you don't have any appointments or hearings?" Dr. Tall and Broody asks.

"No."

"Good, neither do I."

"And why do I care?"

"Because it means you have time to discuss your daughter's request to meet her father."

The elevator doors ding open, and he marches out without waiting for a reply.

Sixteen

Lucas

I cross the narrow hall, unlock my door, and theatrically show the inside to Medusa, letting Miss Attorney know she's not getting out of this conversation.

Looking prissy enough, and kind of sexy in her uniform of a tight pencil skirt suit—mauve today—she walks into the office. And I can't help but wonder what shade of lace she's wearing underneath those clothes. Does she keep an array of panties in different shades of pink, same as with the purple suits?

Okay. I seriously need to find a way to de-sexualize Vivian. I can't be having these kinds of unprofessional thoughts while counseling someone.

Patient's mother, patient's mother, I chant in my head.

"Please take a seat wherever you're most comfortable," I say.

Vivian eyes the sofa with disdain. "I'm not sitting on the cuckoo couch."

"I'm a psychologist," I clarify. "Not a psychiatrist. Struggling couples hardly qualify as *cuckoo.*" Although that might not apply to all my cases, to be fair.

"Still not sitting there," Medusa says, slumping in one of the armchairs facing my desk.

I drop my briefcase on the floor and sit at my desk. Time to switch to professional mode and forget my grievances with this woman. If my forehead were a screen, the words *mother of a patient in need* would be flashing across and hopefully sink into the brain behind.

"Thank you for being here," I say.

Medusa raises a skeptical eyebrow, as if to say, *"You didn't give me much of a choice."*

"I know you're uncomfortable discussing Tegan's father," I continue, "and it mustn't be any easier to do so with me, but I can assure you our personal history has nothing to do with what I am about to say. Nor will it influence in any way my advice."

Medusa still stays silent; the only giveaway she's nervous comes from the shoe—black patent leather, red sole, stiletto heel, too sexy, too distracting—she keeps tapping on the floor.

"As you know, Tegan sought my help after the vodka incident—"

"Did she tell you why she did it?"

"Yes, but I'm not at liberty to discuss—"

"She must like one of the boys. A mother can tell…"

"As I said, I can't share any details besides what Tegan has given me permission to divulge." Medusa scoffs. I ignore her and move on. "Anyway, while we were discussing the vodka debacle, Tegan brought up her father—"

"Really, how? What's the connection between the two?"

I swear, if she interrupts me one more time… I pinch my nose and try to remain calm. Air in. Air out.

"I asked what her dad thought about the incident, and Tegan told me she doesn't know who her father is, which unraveled a whole new discussion about how you refuse to tell her who he is."

Medusa gives me a long, piercing stare. "So, technically, *you* brought up Tegan's father."

I might be sitting on the chair behind the desk, but Vivian is making it clear she's in charge and handling me like a hostile witness.

"It doesn't matter how the topic came up, what matters is—"

"I disagree. Seems to me that if you hadn't stuck your nose into things that are none of your business, we wouldn't be having this conversation at all."

"Maybe not, but your daughter would still want to know who her father is, and you'd still be doing your best to pretend the topic is a non-issue while it matters a great deal to Tegan."

We stand on our respective sides of the desk, glaring at each other. This exchange is getting way too confrontational. I need to restore the calm so we can continue the discussion in civil tones.

I struggle not to flare my nostrils and put my hands forward in what I hope is perceived as a calming gesture. "Just to be clear, I'm not accusing you of anything, or implying you did something wrong."

"Really? Because you're coming across as an awful lot judgmental right now."

"Sorry, that's not my intention."

"What do you want from me, then?"

"Tegan has expressed a serious interior struggle about not knowing where half of her comes from, one that might fall in a blind spot for you because of your own"—I put my hands forward again to show this is not a critique—"feelings toward the man in question. I'm sure you have valid reasons for not wanting to expose Tegan to this man. To protect your daughter from someone you're certain would only bring her more pain. Was he…" I don't know how to phrase this. "… a violent man?"

Medusa's eyes widen. "Gosh, no. Nothing like that. Just a selfish prick."

We stare at each other for the longest time, and I swear my breath was more even at the end of my eight-mile run earlier this morning.

The tension breaks when my phone rings, piercing the loaded silence.

I take it out of my briefcase and check the ID: *Listen to Your Heart.*

Yeah, right. Just what I need now, a call from my damn Dating Specialist. I silence the phone and put it on "do not disturb."

"Sorry," I apologize to Medusa. "I usually turn it off before a session, but this wasn't exactly planned."

Vivian waves me off in an *it's okay* way, just as my landline rings.

"Sorry," I repeat. "This line is for emergencies; a client might need me. Do you mind if I pick up?"

"Go ahead," she says, still a little stiff.

"Hello," I say into the receiver.

"Good morning, Dr. Keller, this is Jennifer, your Dating Specialist from *Listen to Your Heart.*"

I pinch my nose; the woman is a Rottweiler. "Morning, Jennifer," I reply, annoyed. "I stated in my questionnaire this number was for emergencies only."

"Well, Dr. Keller, your dating life *is* an emergency."

And from the little smirk now tugging at Medusa's lips, it's obvious she can hear both sides of the conversation.

"This isn't a good moment. Can I call you back?"

"Are you in session?"

"Not exactly, but—"

"Don't worry, then, this will take only a few minutes," Jennifer insists. "I have the morning booked solid with appointments, and I need to collect feedback on Saturday night to present to Miss Bishop as soon as possible." Why is she still using our aliases, I wonder, as the tirade continues. "It wouldn't be gentlemanlike to make a lady wait. I'll be quick, I promise."

"Go ahead," I surrender, sagging backward in my chair. Medusa is staring at me with an amused glint in her eyes. From the looks of it, I'd say Vivian is going to enjoy the next five minutes just as much as I'm going to hate them.

"Very well, Dr. Keller," Jennifer continues. "I'm happy to inform you Miss Bishop has expressed an interest in going on a second date with you. Did you find her to be a suitable match?"

"No," I reply curtly.

"Oh, may I ask why?"

I sigh, looking at Medusa again. At least she knows already. "Because, mid-date, Meadow declared she's a witch."

"Hold on just a second…"

The sound of paper shuffling comes through the line. "Yes, I can see from Miss Bishop's questionnaire she has an esoteric faith." More paper rustling. "But you also stated in your questionnaire that you didn't care about a potential partner's denomination."

"Yeah, well, I didn't anticipate that would include women who are convinced they can perform magic spells."

I make the mistake of looking at Medusa again; she's not

even trying to hide her smile.

"I'm sorry, but how is one belief more legitimate than another, Dr. Keller? Don't all religions rely on blind faith?"

Medusa raises her eyebrow at me in a, *I want to see you get out of this one* way. I ignore her silent provocation and reply to Jennifer. "Listen, I'd rather not debate theological arguments with you. Just, please, no more witches."

"Noted. Was religion the only issue with Miss Bishop? She stated you ended the date quite abruptly."

"I had my reasons," I say.

"What reasons?"

"Those are private."

"Sorry, Dr. Keller, but if you want this process to work, you need to be forthcoming. Why did you leave?"

Vivian tilts her head as if saying, *something to hide, Doctor?*

"Meadow… err… propositioned me in a way I wasn't comfortable with."

"What made you uncomfortable?" Jennifer asks.

Medusa's grin turns evil at this point.

I stare right back at Vivian and say, "Meadow asked me point-blank to have sex with her."

Medusa doesn't drop her gaze, but is that a faint blush on her cheeks?

"And that was a problem because…?" On the line, the familiar rustling of paper comes back. "You stated on your questionnaire that sexuality is an important aspect of a relationship for you. Are you uncomfortable getting physical with a partner?"

Vivian raises that mocking eyebrow again, and I hope *I'm* not blushing as I spit my answer between gritted teeth. "Only when the act is intended as a propitiatory rite to harness the Earth's power in anticipation of a scrying ritual to take place at midnight."

"Okay," Jennifer says, nonplussed. "Your objections have been noted, Dr. Keller, and we'll keep your feedback in mind when selecting your next match. I wish you a great day, and remember, true love is only one date away." She singsongs the last part.

"A good day to you, too." I slam the receiver down and raise a warning finger toward Medusa. "Not a word."

Vivian throws her head back and finally laughs openly until her eyes glisten with tears. "I'm sorry," she says between chuckles. "What a *charming* night you must've had." The laughter continues. "Makes my Saturday look not so bad in comparison."

She's beautiful when she laughs. The realization hits me unbidden. To be fair, Vivian has always been a good-looking woman, but without the usual aura of austerity and disdain, I see her in a whole different light. A dangerous, too-attractive one. She must sense I'm staring at her funny, because her mirth slowly disappears.

"What?" she asks.

I rake a hand through my hair. "Nothing," I say. "I hope at least one day my future wife and I will laugh the whole thing off. It'll be a great story to tell our grandkids: that time grandpa went on a date with a witch."

It's Medusa's turn to stare at me as if she was seeing me for the first time.

"Yeah," she agrees. "It'll make for a good story."

We share another serious look, maybe even a silent agreement to lay down our arms.

But, contrary to my optimistic feelings, Vivian stiffens in her chair and checks her watch, asking, "Are we done yet? I don't have all morning."

And, just like that, the comradeship is gone and we're back on opposite sides of the fence. "Sorry, no. We still need to discuss Tegan's father." We've circled the issue enough, so I go ahead with a direct question. "Why do you refuse to disclose his identity?"

Medusa stares daggers at me. "Do I have to answer?"

"You don't *have* to do anything. If you're not comfortable talking to me, I can refer you to a colleague, but you *should* address the issue. For your daughter's sake."

Vivian stares at the floor, nibbles nervously at a fingernail, and then scoffs, exasperated. "I can't believe I'm sharing the story with you, my sworn enemy."

"Oh, come on, would a sworn enemy almost break his neck so you wouldn't miss a hearing?" I had to throw my IOU card in there eventually.

She takes a deep breath. "When I got pregnant, I was a freshman at Harvard. Tegan's father was my English Literature TA. I was eighteen, he was twenty-seven—smart, handsome, with that literary artist halo... I fell for him during the first lecture, but never expected my feelings to be reciprocated. Long story short, we started a clandestine relationship, as he couldn't openly date a student. I was so in love with him." Vivian shakes her head, and her mouth thins in that hard line she's shown me so many times. "When I found out about the pregnancy, I was scared, but I thought we'd raise the baby together, get married, start a family. Like the naïve child I was, I told him everything with a big smile on my face." Her voice cracks at this point.

"And he refused to accept his responsibilities?"

"Oh, not just that. He went on a rampage, called me a liar, saying that I was trying to trap him, ruin his career, accusing me of going off the pill on purpose. I hadn't. Tegan is really the product of a carton of leftovers gone bad and a night spent throwing up in my dorm bathroom. It never occurred to me that vomiting a single pill could nullify the effect of the whole box, but it did."

I sense she's still withholding information. "Is raging all the professor did?"

We hold gazes for the longest time. Then, Vivian confirms my suspicions. "No," she says. "He said he wasn't interested in being a father, that the baby probably wasn't even his, and that I should get rid of it before anyone found out. When I refused, he demanded I transfer to a different school, and threatened to fail me in both his classes if I didn't comply."

I realize I'm gripping the armrests of my chair only when I have to pry my fingers away. The man sounds like a prime asshole.

"And you didn't report him to the faculty board?"

Vivian shakes her head. "I was eighteen, scared, alone, heartbroken. I was lost. So, I did everything he asked: I finished the semester at Harvard before my belly showed and transferred to Columbia the next year. I wouldn't have been able to raise a kid on my own and still graduate while in Boston, anyway." She shrugs. "At least in New York my parents could help."

"The professor sounds like a real piece of work," I say.

"Yeah, right?"

"Sort of makes me want to go on a second date with the

witch just so I can ask her to curse him."

Vivian smiles. A saddish, bittersweet smile, but a smile nonetheless. "Yeah," she agrees. "I'd like to see that. But you get why I don't want Tegan to meet him. That man is toxic."

"I do…"

"I sense a 'but' coming."

"*But* Tegan is no longer a child. It should be her decision. Are you more afraid he'll refuse to be in her life, or that he will want to be part of it?"

"Both options seem equally dreadful, and neither will do Tegan any good."

"To the contrary: both would."

"Really? How?"

"If he wants nothing to do with her, Tegan will stop blaming you for keeping her away from her other parent. It'll hurt at first, sure. But it'll also give Tegan closure and allow her to heal. And if, instead, he ends up regretting his choice, Tegan will have a chance to meet her father. Fifteen years is a long time for a man to reflect on his mistakes. He could regret his decision."

"Yeah? Then why didn't he try to find his daughter *once* in all these years? I'm not that hard to track down."

"I can't answer that question. Only he can. Do you know where he is now?"

Vivian lets out a bitter scoff. "Dean of Arts and Humanities at Harvard. A few months ago, I came across an article somewhere about the *youngest faculty member ever appointed to the position.* I never said he wasn't smart… or driven."

"Okay," I say. "Then the only remaining question is: are you ready to share all this with Tegan?"

Seventeen

Vivian

Dr. Magnanimous agrees to let me stew for a few days on what we discussed. Still, the conversation leaves me kind of raw. In my office, I try to concentrate on a deposition but fail miserably. When my phone rings, I welcome the distraction.

"Hello. This is Vivian Hessington."

"Hi, Miss Hessington, this is Barbara, your Dating Specialist from *Listen to Your Heart.* Can you talk now?"

"Yes, I'm not with a client."

"Great, because I have good news. The agency has found a new match for you. Would you be free this upcoming weekend?"

"Yes," I confirm. Provided my daughter doesn't get deeper into her teenage rebellion phase.

"Perfect. I'll inform your match and let you know as soon as he picks a location and time."

"Okay, fantastic. I'll wait for your call."

***

The date ends up being a Sunday brunch at Robert, a classic New York spot. The restaurant is nestled atop the Museum of Arts & Design and overlooks Columbus Circle and Central Park. I've only been once, but always wanted to come back. The view from the top is amazing.

I enter the iconic New York building through the glass revolving door, ignore the museum admission booth, and head straight for the elevator. There are no mirrors on the elevator walls, but I still try to check my reflection in the silver plates of the sliding doors as it carries me up to the ninth floor.

Even through the distortion, I'm happy with what I see. My dress is new—teal silk, knee-length, with peekaboo shoulders—and so are the suede magenta pumps. Plus, Tegan curled my hair and spent close to an hour meticulously following a "Perfect First Date Makeup" tutorial on YouTube. My daughter has assured me I'm channeling all the right "Taylor Swift at the 2015 Grammys" vibes.

When I reach the top floor, I give the hostess the alias Barbara gave me for my mystery man—Mr. Tolstoy. The woman's eyes widen slightly at the uncommon-but-famous name and directs me to our table—a window one! True, we're in the second row, but this place must get busy on Sundays, especially since I saw it mentioned in Eater New York recently in a piece about restaurants with stunning views. Maybe that's where my date got the idea to have lunch here.

I'm admiring the beautiful views of Central Park when the hostess comes back to show a man to the table next door—the one closer to the windows. He thanks the woman, sits, and our eyes meet.

Mine narrow, while his widen.

"*You*," I say. "What are you doing here?"

"I'm on a blind date. You?"

"Same."

Lucas gives me a once over, taking his time, his gaze resting on my shoes longer than is polite. I wiggle my ankle pointedly.

His eyes snap back up, and he coughs. "Yeah, I can see that. You're less... I mean more... err..."

Dr. Keller never finishes the phrase, changing the subject instead. "Should I ask for a different table?"

A quick scan of the restaurant reveals all the window tables are occupied—both rows.

I'm about to tell him "don't bother," when the hostess comes back once again, leading a pretty blonde to his table—she's young, under thirty for sure.

Lucas stands up at once, and they greet with an awkward side hug. They exchange names—Luke, Sonia, nice to meet you—and he helps her sit down.

"Err," Shrek coughs, visibly embarrassed. "Is this table okay, or would you prefer to move away from the windows—lots of light here," he adds, eyeing one of the free tables in the back of the room.

Poor guy, he really doesn't want to have his date while sitting next to me, and can I blame him?

"Oh, no," Sonia says. "Light is so important for people's wellbeing; otherwise, they decompose."

I almost choke on a sip of water. I look up at Lucas; he's staring at his date, frowning.

"Decompose?"

"Yeah, you know, when they get all mopey and sad."

"You mean they get *depressed?*"

"Yes, I just told you. It's why suicides spike in France when they have entire months without sunlight."

"Err... Finland, perhaps?"

Sonia waves him off. "Yeah, like, Europe, whatever." Then she grabs a glass, fills it with water, and drains the contents in a few long drags. "Sorry, I'm dehydrated. I went to my college's five-year reunion last night and got a little carried away with the drinks."

"Ehm, okay?" Dr. You're-So-Losing-Our-Bet unfolds his napkin on his lap and gives me the evil, don't-you-dare-mock-me-about-this eye. I make an innocent face. Luke ignores me and goes back to looking at his date. "Where did you go to college?"

"NYU. You?"

"Stanford, for my bachelor and master degrees," he says. "And then Berkley for my doctoral. For my post-doc, I was a fellow at Michigan."

Show off, I mutter to myself. But Sonia has an opposite reaction. She gasps loudly, asking, "Oh my gosh, what did you do?"

"What do you mean?"

"Why did you wind up at Michigan?"

Uncertainly, Lucas replies, "Uh, for a research study on youth transitional age, but then I specialized in couples' counseling."

Sonia sits back in her chair. "And they sent you to prison for that?"

"Prison? No, what...?" The puzzled look on Shrek's face turns to exasperation as his brain clicks. "I said fellow, not felon."

"No, it's okay," Sonia reassures him. "I understand if you prefer not to talk about the time you spent in jail. It couldn't have been easy."

And I swear I have to turn my head not to laugh in his face. I stare at my watch and note that no matter how weird Lucas' date is, at least she was on time. Mine is already ten minutes late. Oh crap, what if I got stood up? That'd be bad enough on its own, but to be blown off in front of Shrek would be disastrous. A catastrophe.

Feeling a lot less smug, I stare back at the restaurant entrance and sigh in relief when I see the same hostess from before heading my way with a tall man in tow.

They reach me a minute later. The hostess smiles and leaves, giving me my first unobstructed view of the guy the agency selected as my potential Mr. Right.

Mmm.

Mr. Tolstoy is tall, but more in a lanky way than hunky. His hair is unruly and on the longish side, and while the style might've worked for him a few years ago, it doesn't anymore now that his hair is thinning out. He's wearing a pair of dark jeans, scruffy leather shoes, and a white shirt that either has not been ironed or that has been worn too long already. The pale-blue linen suit jacket that completes the outfit is equally wrinkled, and is that a coffee stain over his breast pocket?

I try to keep an open mind and get up to greet him with a smile.

"Hi," I say. "I'm Vivian."

He clasps my hand in a clammy handshake. "Christopher. Sorry I'm late, but I got lost in a creative bubble. You know how it gets."

Actually, I don't know, since we've never met. Is he a painter?

"It's okay," I say as we both sit. "Are you an artist?"

As Christopher unfolds his napkin and places it on his lap, I try not to notice how my date seems to be the store-brand package compared to the name-brand sitting next door. His hair a drab, mousy brown to Lucas' lustrous, glossy black locks. The clothes a poor replica of Lucas' pristine white dress-shirt and shiny Italian leather shoes. Even their eyes are the same color: blue. But Lucas' are deep and vibrant, while Christopher's are a vapid, transparent color and red-rimmed like an old man's.

But, I remind myself, the package is of little importance. I've already witnessed firsthand how misleading appearances can be with my reverse-ogre of a neighbor. So, I won't judge a book by its cover, and I'll keep an open mind.

I stare at Christopher with a friendly smile, waiting for his answer. He finishes smoothing the creases out of the napkin on his lap with a bit too much flare, and finally looks up at me.

"I'm a writer," he says with self-importance. "An artist of the written word."

"Wow. That's amazing. Have you published many books?"

"No, I'm not trying to be a commercial bestseller. I create literary art. That requires time."

"Oh, okay, what do you write about?"

"It's not so much *what* as it is *how*. The craftsmanship that goes behind sedulously assembling words to produce a harmonious symphony of text."

Sedulou—what? Could this guy be any more pretentious?

Thank goodness the monolog is interrupted by a server arriving to take our order. I had plenty of time to study the menu, and I was set on getting an appetizer and the risotto, but I have a hunch I'll want to cut this date as short as possible. "French toast, please," I order. Sugar is my friend.

"Anything to drink?" the server asks me.

Yeah, alcohol could help, too. "A Bellini, please."

The server jots my preferences in his pad and turns to

Christopher.

The next great American novelist is studying the menu, his nose upturned as if smelling something unpleasant.

I watch him, the server watches him, but he keeps staring at the, frankly, limited brunch menu, as if he had to choose the right word for one of his precious manuscripts. After what seems like forever, he finally raises an unimpressed stare to our waiter, saying, "I'll take the rib eye steak and eggs, and a glass of your best red."

The server walks away, leaving me once again alone with Mr. Tolstoy Wannabe. I hope at least they'll be quick in bringing our drinks. My gaze unwisely drifts sideways toward Lucas. Our eyes meet for a brief second, and he winks at me before returning his attention to his date.

The little gesture makes me blush, and causes my stomach to do a silly, unwarranted flip.

Oh, gosh. Where is that drink?

Eighteen

Lucas

After casually eavesdropping on Medusa's date for a while, I feel secure in my professional housing situation. No way Vivian will go out with that pompous windbag a second time. Not if she has an ounce of sanity in her. Unfortunately, my own date isn't going much better.

"What do you do for a living?" I ask Sonia.

Not because I care, but to keep a basic conversation flowing until the meal is over and I can politely excuse myself. Once again, I'm in the middle of a date with a woman I have no interest in seeing again. Sonia's constant word confusing is annoying—but that alone wouldn't have been enough to toss her in the "never again" box. But she's kept her phone on the table the entire time we've been seated and hasn't gone more than ten seconds without checking it. A huge no-no for me. She probably doesn't understand half of what I say because she's only partially listening to me between composing texts.

To prove my point, Sonia finishes typing something on her phone before answering my question. "I'm a lifestyle blogger. At least, that's how my business started. Today, you might call me an 'influencer.'" She air-quotes the last word.

"Is it a difficult job?" I ask.

"Not so much once you have a solid base of followers, but I constantly have to engage with them on all my socials."

"Sounds demanding."

"Exactly," Sonia says. "Many people don't understand,

135

but I'm glad you get it. And I'm lucky I haven't had to deal with too many trolls so far. People can be mean online."

"Oh, trust me, people can be dreadful also in real life."

"Sorry, you're right, I can only imagine what awful things you saw in prison."

Before I have a chance to reply, her ten free seconds expire and she picks up her phone again.

Whatever, I give up.

Constantly being connected is part of her livelihood, I get it, and I have nothing against it per se, but it'd drive me crazy in a relationship.

While Sonia is busy, my attention is inevitably pulled back to the other couple having an awful first date.

"How's your steak?" Medusa asks.

"Rather ligneous," the windbag replies. "Overcooked."

Ah, from the way he's scarfing the food down, I wouldn't have guessed.

The literary artist doesn't ask Vivian about her dish, but she tells him anyway. "Really? Strange, because the French toast is delicious."

A loud ringtone rips through the quiet chattering of the restaurant. Windbag, unperturbed, takes his time wiping his mouth on his napkin before he retrieves the ringing phone from his jeans pocket.

"Apologies," he says. "It's my agent; I have to get this. It could be important news."

Christopher gets up and leaves the main room to go talk somewhere more private. Medusa doesn't appear heartbroken to be abandoned halfway through her date; on the contrary, she seems relieved.

I keep looking at her, but she pointedly avoids my gaze,

downs the rest of her drink, and then orders another one.

Ignored by Medusa, I turn back to Sonia, and find her moving her wine glass around the table while taking several shots of it with the view of Central Park in the background. I politely wait a good five minutes until she's done.

Photos taken, she looks up at me. "Thank you for picking this place for our date, it's so photogenic. I'll be able to post a great Insta story."

"Sure," I say, thinking my Dating Specialist and I will have to have a serious conversation on their selection process.

Sonia's phone pings on the table. She checks it, and her eyes widen.

"Dude," she says. "A friend just texted me about an Angelika Black flash sale happening two blocks away. Do you mind if I scram? My followers will go nuts for it, and lunch is over anyway."

I sigh. I would've offered to pay the bill, but for the gesture to be taken for granted irks me a little. At least, with her swift departure, there won't be any pretense of a second date happening.

"Not at all," I say.

"You're the best." She collects her things and gets up.

I stand up as well. No matter that she's being—quite frankly—rude, I won't let my good manners be compromised.

Sonia circles the table and gives me a boisterous hug, saying, "Thanks, this has been amazing, can't wait to do it again."

The declaration leaves me a little speechless. This is her idea of a great date? What happens on bad ones, I wonder.

When I don't reply, she looks at me with a weird intensity in her eyes and gives me a second, longer hug.

Another squeeze and she finally lets go. I look at her a bit baffled, asking, "Are you okay?"

"I am," she says. "The question is, *are you?*"

I gape, unsure how to reply.

Sonia must take my silence as a sign I'm not okay, because she continues. "If you still have nightmares about what happened to you in prison, you should download my friend Audrey's mental health app. I'll send you the link."

I've given up by this point on convincing her I never went to prison. But Sonia casually recommending a mental health app to who knows how many followers worries me. "Is your friend a certified professional?"

"Yeah, of course. I wouldn't recommend her app otherwise."

"Is she a colleague?"

"No," Sonia scoffs. "Audrey didn't go to college. As if going to some big-name school gives you a license to tell people what to do with their lives! Besides, Audrey's max zen—she's the best yoga instructor in New York. I can't believe you haven't heard of her."

Evidently, Sonia missed the part where I told her I was a psychologist. I'm starting to doubt she heard much of anything that came out of my mouth. "I wouldn't trust mental health issues to someone without a degree," I warn. "And neither should your followers."

"Audrey's app is more about working on yourself through self-consciousness and meditation. I'll send you the link, but sorry, I have to go now if I want to catch anything decent at that sale. All the best items disappear in the first ten minutes.

You wouldn't believe what a jungle it is out there."

To avoid being pity-hugged again, I take a step back and wish her good luck with the flash sale.

Once Sonia is gone, I slump down in my seat, mentally exhausted after that disaster of a date. Once I recover, I search the room for a server to ask for the bill. I catch one's gaze and make a pen-writing-on-paper gesture. He nods at me, letting me know he understood.

I risk a glance at Vivian, and am surprised to find her staring right back, a poorly concealed half-smile pulling at her lips. Medusa can't resist; she wrinkles her nose and gives me a mocking double thumbs up.

I ignore the provocation and look away, still waiting for that server. The sooner I can leave, the better.

In the meantime, her companion returns and sits back at the table, just as their bill arrives. Medusa must've asked for it while I was saying goodbye to Sonia. Guess she's as eager as me to get out of here.

Windbag looks at the check, but makes no move to take it, so Vivian, with a forced smile, grabs the leather folder, declaring, "Let's split it, shall we?"

"By all means, I'm not paying for this excrementitious meal on my own."

Vivian's face falls while her cheeks color, and it's my turn to silently laugh.

"The steak was thirty dollars," the literary artist continues, taking his wallet out of his pocket.

Thirty-*one* dollars, Mr. Cheap, I correct him in my head.

He produces a twenty and a ten and drops them on the table. "For my part."

Vivian raises an eyebrow, probably wondering if the man

simply forgot about taxes, the tip, and the glass of "the restaurant's best red" he ordered, or if the windbag isn't just a literary artist but also a shakedown pro. I'd say the second. And from the taut curve of her lips, I assume Medusa must've come to the same conclusion. Now, another question poses itself before her: to argue and make the windbag fork his real half of the bill, or shell out a few more bucks and be rid of the cockroach at once?

Vivian's nostrils flare, but she bites her tongue, saying nothing.

I can't help but notice the fleeting flash of triumph crossing Mr. Novelist's face. He must think himself quite the clever man, when in reality he's the joke.

Christopher the Cheap grabs his jacket from the back of his chair and comes to stand next to Vivian.

"Sorry, there was no chemistry between us. These arranged trysts don't always work out. But I had a very pleasant time with you, Vivian. I'll send you a link to buy my book when it comes out. Have a lovely day."

And with that closing line, he waltzes out of the restaurant.

Medusa's reaction is to glare at me as if daring me to say or do anything. And, I know I'm being petty, but I can't help but return the grimacing thumbs-up gesture.

We pay for our bills at the same time and share an elevator ride downstairs.

Medusa stares at me, clearly dying to say something.

I groan and snap, "Come on, spit it out."

She tilts her head, giving me a fake-innocent smile. "I was just trying to picture you wearing a bright orange jumpsuit."

"My date might've had trouble confusing terms, but at

least she didn't use every single word she knew every time she spoke. And the performance that windbag put up not to pay for his fair share of the meal was stellar. Guess he was really invested in living up to the struggling artist stereotype."

"At least my date paid for *some* of the meal. Thirty bucks is better than nothing; yours was a total freeloader."

We're still arguing as we exit the museum and step on the curb outside.

I eye her high heels dubiously. "Are you taking a cab home?" I ask her, realizing for the first time that I have no idea where she lives. Is she in Manhattan like me, or Brooklyn, or somewhere else entirely?

"Yup," she says. "I'm not walking in these." She wiggles a foot at me.

"Didn't think so," I say, trying not to get distracted by the magenta stiletto. My deranged brain at once wonders if her underwear matches the dress, or the heels, or neither. I swear, one glimpse of lace has doomed me for life.

Out of the corner of my eye, I catch an empty cab coming our way, and raise my arm before she can.

When the taxi stops next to us, I open the door before Vivian can object and wave at her to get inside. Whatever her idea of me, I'm not uncivil. I had exactly one slip-up the first time we met, and now she'll hold that single, stress-fueled moment of bad temper against me forever.

Medusa seems surprised by my kind gesture as she gets into the car. "Thank you," she says. And then she has to ruin it by adding, "Bye-bye, inmate."

And, poor manners or not, before closing the door on her, I hiss, "I wish you a rather excrementitious rest of your day."

Nineteen

Vivian

The cab's door slams shut, and I can't help smiling. The man, if nothing else, makes me laugh. I tell the driver my address and, as the car pulls into the street, I give a brooding Lucas a little wave through the window.

I'd be hard-pressed to decide which date was worse: mine, or his. But I keep laughing in my head throughout the entire cab ride as I remember snippets of his conversation with Sonia. If not for Lucas, lunch would've been utterly cheerless. Misery truly loves company.

At home, the moment I unlock the door, I'm welcomed by an avalanche of teenage angst. Tegan launches into my arms with a tear-streaked face, wailing, "Mom!"

All the worst-case scenarios shuffle through my brain at once: cyberbullying, alcohol again, Tegan's pregnant...

"What?" I ask, agitated. "What happened?"

"Priscilla," Tegan says. "She's gone! I swear I left the door open only for a second, because I didn't have enough change to pay the delivery guy, and she must've slipped through. But by the time I noticed, I couldn't find her anywhere. I've asked all our neighbors, but no one has seen her."

Okay, an MIA cat I can deal with.

"Don't worry, honey," I say, hugging her to my chest. "Priscilla has her collar with our address and phone number. I'm sure someone will find her."

"But Prissy has never been out on her own. What if

142

something happens to her?"

"Let me get changed, and we can go look for her. Why don't you print a flyer with her picture, and we'll make copies at the shop around the corner and distribute them around the neighborhood."

"On it, Mom, you go get changed. Be quick. We can't lose any more time."

***

After an afternoon spent plastering our block with pictures of our missing cat, Tegan and I come back home tired and miserable and still cat-less, only to find the lost feline impatiently waiting for us on the front steps. Priscilla stares us down, swaying her tail back and forth as if annoyed we're late for her usual dinnertime.

Tegan doesn't seem to mind the cat's airs, and rushes to scoop her into her arms. "Prissy!"

The cat is further rewarded for her disappearing act with a shower of kisses.

Shaking my head, I herd both cat and human into the house, where the three of us spend the evening snuggled on the couch watching a romantic movie and just plain appreciating being together.

But I can't concentrate on the plot. My attention keeps drifting to Tegan and the way she's holding Priscilla tight to her chest and cuddling the cat non-stop. And I can't help but wonder if her reaction today was normal. Yes, people get attached to their pets and consider them almost human, like a member of the family. But Tegan was desperate, anguished, grief-stricken. A hard question pops into my head: does Tegan have abandonment issues?

I reflect on everything Lucas and I discussed. Like it or not, he *is* a good therapist, and even if I don't want to admit it, he might have a better insight into what troubles my daughter a month after knowing her than I do after a lifetime spent together.

He was right when he said Tegan's father is a giant blind spot for me. But not anymore. I purse my lips and make a decision: time to tell Tegan who her father is. But, how?

I mentally scoff when I come to the realization that the best person to ask for advice is none other than Shrink Shrek.

***

Tegan still has another week of early morning detention, so the next day, I beat Shrek to the office and wait for him to show up outside his door.

Lucas steps out of the elevator twenty minutes later, as impeccably dressed as always and just as annoyingly good looking.

"Finally," I greet him. "I thought I'd have to wait here all morning."

He scowls at finding me guarding his ogre's lair. "I'm sorry, did we have an appointment I forgot about?"

Dr. Ogre unlocks his door and I follow him inside the office. "We do now."

"Why, no, you aren't getting in the way of an appointment I already have scheduled," he says sarcastically.

"You never schedule a session before ten a.m.," I retort.

His ridiculously blue eyes widen. "Have you been secretly keeping tabs on me?"

"I'm just observant."

Lucas takes his seat behind the desk, showing me the

same armchair as last time. "Please make yourself at home." He crosses his hands on the table. "To what do I owe this unexpected pleasure?"

I sit and get straight to the point. "I want to tell Tegan about her father."

All the sarcasm evaporates from Lucas' features, and he becomes immediately serious but smiley, if that's even a thing. "Good," he says. "It's the right choice. When do you want to tell her?"

"Oh no, not me. *You*'re going to do it."

"Me?"

"Tegan is coming to see you this afternoon, right?"

"Yes."

"Tell her after you're done with your"—I make a flapping hand gesture—"shrinking."

"I'm not a psychiatrist," Mr. I Got My Bachelor and Master at Stanford corrects me. "And why don't you want to tell her yourself?"

I hate that I have to show my vulnerable side to Lucas, but somehow, deep down, I also feel that I can trust him with my innermost secrets. "When it comes to *that man*—see? I can't even bring myself to say his name—I don't trust my gut reaction. I could get mad, spew evil, change my mind as I talk... I can't do that to Tegan."

Lucas stares at me for a long time before saying, "It's good to know our limits, and there's no shame in asking for help." And with a cheeky grin, he adds, "Even if you hate asking *me*."

And he's charmed me into smiling. "So, Doctor, how do you want to proceed?"

"I'll talk with Tegan this afternoon and then, if you're

145

okay with it, I'd like to bring you in for a controlled discussion with both of you."

"Right." The thought sounds terrifying, but I have no choice. "What should I tell Tegan about how things went down sixteen years ago? Everything? Nothing?"

Lucas leans back in his chair, thinking hard. Eventually, he says, "Let it be her choice how much she wants to know. If she wishes to rebuild a relationship with her father, it could be better if they started with a clean slate. He might be a very different man now."

Now I'm positively cringing. The thought of Tegan going anywhere near that man makes my stomach tighten with so many knots I want to puke. I imagine them in the same dusty office where I used to meet him for our clandestine hookups—which doesn't make any sense, because a dean will have been upgraded to a much grander space than a TA. But in my head, it's how I picture the encounter, and the mental image makes me dizzy on top of being nauseated.

Lucas takes in my reaction, and his features soften in a way I've never seen before. It's impossible to reconcile this side of him with the lunatic who barged into my office the day I signed the lease, yelling about stolen donuts and other nonsense.

"I know this is hard on you," he says in a soft, low voice that sounds like honey. "But you're doing the right thing for Tegan. You're a wonderful mother."

His words spread over me like a warm blanket, but this conversation is already cutting too deep. So I don't let on I appreciate his metaphorical outstretched hand, and slap it away with sarcasm instead. "Careful, Doctor," I say. "That almost sounded like a compliment."

"Maybe because it was," he says, a little cross. "Now if you don't mind." Lucas stands up abruptly. "I have to prepare for my next session."

"Sure."

I follow him to the door.

"Once Tegan arrives for our appointment, I'll give you a call," he tells me.

"You don't have my number."

Shrek's nostrils flare. "Then I'll make the effort of walking six paces to your door and knocking."

"You rattle too easily," I tease him.

Lucas advances a step, towering over me. "It happens only with you," he says, eyes burning into mine.

And a weird, different-kind-of-warm sensation spreads in my belly, which is my cue to flee his office and go hide in mine. As I slam my door shut and lean back against it, I'm definitely not thinking about how blue his eyes are, or how soft his hair looks, or how good it would feel to rake my hand through it and pull his head down to—yep, definitely not thinking about any of that.

***

By the time the hour of Tegan's appointment arrives, I'm staring at my laptop, furiously biting my nails while trying not to chew them off. They were supposed to meet five minutes ago. How long will it take before Lucas calls me in? How will Tegan react?

By four-thirty, I'm pacing behind my door like a caged animal. When Lucas finally knocks fifteen minutes later, I'm so quick answering that I find him with his hand still raised, ready for a second knock.

147

He drops the arm, takes one look at me, and says, "Relax."

I point a finger at him. "You mother a daughter alone for fifteen years and then have to agree to let her meet her scumbag father and only *then* tell me to *relax*."

I'm about to march past him to go hug my daughter, but he grabs me by the shoulders, gently but firmly. Lucas stares right into my eyes, saying, "What I meant was, you can't go in there looking like you're about to hyperventilate. You've been the single most important person in Tegan's life since she was born, and she already feels guilty about..." He hesitates. "...needing more."

Lucas' words stab me straight in the heart. The thought that, no matter how hard I try, I'm not enough for my daughter has been tormenting me ever since the meet-the-estranged-father drama started. "But you're doing this for her," Lucas continues. "And she needs to know you're on board. Take two deep breaths. I promise, it'll help."

Still holding me with both hands, he waits for me to comply. I do.

"Let the tension from your shoulders go," Lucas continues, giving my upper arms a gentle rub. "Take a deep breath in..."

He keeps guiding me through some relaxation techniques, and I try to follow his instructions, but honestly, I'm more distracted by the deep sound of his voice, the way his lips move, the touch of his hands on my arms... And why do his eyes have to be so blue?

And shouldn't this exercise make my breathing even? It's getting more ragged by the minute—and the fast pace has nothing to do with anxiety.

Lucas must pick up on the weird vibe, because he lets me go and takes a step back, coughing out an embarrassed, "You good?"

"Yep," I say, still a bit out of breath but at least no longer ridden with nerves. "All good here."

I straighten my jacket and walk across the hall and into his office.

The moment I step in, Tegan barrels into me, hugging me tightly. "Thank you, Mom."

I caress her hair like I used to do when she was little. "Shhh, it's okay." Emotions threaten to overwhelm me, but I don't get the comfort of holding on to my daughter any longer because she lets go and bounces around the room, clapping her hands. "I'm finally going to meet my dad!"

Lucas, in the meantime, has followed me in and is back to sitting in his shrink chair. And for once, I give in and take a seat on the "patient" couch. Tegan flops next to me and I wrap one arm around her waist, pulling her closer.

"How is this going to work?" I ask Lucas.

Tegan answers instead. "We're going to Boston. Dad has agreed to see me outside office hours so I won't lose any more school days."

A ball of acid explodes in my stomach, both at hearing Tegan call that man "Dad" so nonchalantly, and at learning they've already reached out to him without me being present.

I glare at Shrek, trying to stay calm. "You contacted him?"

Once again, Tegan answers. "It was my idea, Mom. And I didn't tell him who I was; I just asked for an appointment. He thinks I'm a prospective student and has agreed to see me."

With a strained smile plastered on my lips, I turn to her. "When?"

"Saturday, two weeks from now."

Over-cheerfully, I say, "I guess we're going to Boston, then."

Tegan's smile falters, and she throws a glance at Lucas and then back at me. "Actually..."

"Yes?" I ask. Whatever she's going to say at this point can't be any worse than the news she's already dropped on me like a lead balloon.

"I'd rather go with Luke."

I was wrong. Rejection hurts every single time. But I keep my features sculpted into a polite smile as I ask, "Why?"

"You and Dad have history, and I don't want this to be about the past and the two of you. I want it to be about me."

"I'm sure Dr. Keller has better things to do with his weekends."

"He's already agreed to take me."

On the one hand, I'm impressed Lucas would go to such lengths for my daughter. Is he like that with all his patients? If so, they're lucky to have him. On the other hand, I can't help but feel like the odd man out. Like they've conspired against me and formed this little secret club I'm not a member of.

"We could've gone this weekend," Tegan continues, oblivious to my inner turmoil, "but Luke already had another date from the agency scheduled."

I have no right to be mad at him. Lucas is helping us, he's going above and beyond whatever might be expected of him professionally. And yet, it feels like my daughter is slipping away from me, a full two and a half years before I was prepared to let her go once she went to college. And since I can't exactly blame Tegan for wanting to meet her father, the only one left to lash out at is her meddling psychologist.

"Another date?" I say. "Wow, you roll through them quickly."

Tegan frowns. "Mom!"

But Lucas completely ignores my sarcasm and simply says, "Jennifer is obsessed with finding me 'the one.' Apparently, I'm a difficult customer and she loves a challenge." His lips part in a self-deprecating and, annoyingly, dashing grin.

I follow his lead and agree to a silent truce. "You mean besides being a difficult neighbor?"

Lucas looks serious now as he asks, "Are you okay with me taking Tegan to Boston?"

What other choice did you leave me? I want to ask.

In his eyes, I read that he's heard me even if I haven't spoken, and he's sorry for blindsiding me with this.

His stare seems to also be telling me: *It's better for your daughter if I go...*

Defeated, I give the only answer left to me. "Yes, you can take her."

This earns me another crushing hug from Tegan.

Over her shoulder, I catch Shrek's eye, letting him know there will be a strict code of conduct on their little trip, and that he will be required to send updates obnoxiously often. Looks like I'll have to give him my phone number after all.

Twenty

Lucas

Saturday night, I'm a little weary as I enter a cute bistro uptown for my third blind date set up by *Listen to Your Heart*. Honestly, I don't have big expectations. A not-too-weird evening would already be a triumph. At this point, I'm not even sure I should keep going on these dates, but the agency fee was exorbitant, so I'd rather find love or get at least a partial refund. And then there's the other thing.

The bet with Medusa.

What if she finds her soulmate before I do?

The thought is disturbing.

Yeah, because it'd mean I'd have to pack my newly set up office.

No. Other. Reason.

Yeah, right, a sarcastic little prick scoffs in my head.

The truth is, lately, Vivian has been on my mind too often. The most random things make me think about her. Like the color pink, which apparently my brain will forever associate with lace and lingerie. Or whenever a client says something funny, I immediately wonder what Vivian would have to say about it. And she has ruined donuts for me forever. If I eat one, I can't help picturing her lips closing with gusto on the glazed sweet the first day I saw her.

And why do I have to think about her every time I go on a date?

Well, last week she was literally sitting at the adjoining table. Okay, but she isn't here tonight—I hope—so there's no need for me to be plagued by her.

At the reception booth, I give my fake name to the hostess and follow her to my table.

My date arrives a few minutes later. A tall woman, with dark auburn hair and brown eyes, who's smiling brightly at me. Carla, she introduces herself. She seems perfectly normal, but I'm not trusting first impressions any longer. I'll wait until the end of the evening to form an opinion.

We order our food. Steak for me, risotto for her—not a dish I'd associate with any magical practice, which is a relief.

When we discuss colleges, she doesn't assume I've been to prison. Another point in her favor.

And then we share what we do for a living. She's a logistics manager for a big company in New Jersey.

So far, so good.

"Have you been on many dates with the agency?" I ask.

"This is my first with *Listen to Your Heart,*" she admits. "I've been with another service before, but it wasn't a good fit."

"Crappy dates?"

"Sort of… Their database was filled with men so narrow-minded. You wouldn't believe how obtuse people can be."

"Yeah, like about what?"

"Take capitalism. I can say without shame that it has flaws. And I'm not a communist or anything, but it's obvious that our economic system isn't perfect, especially after what happened in 2008. Or, you know how some people still refuse to admit that climate change is real…" I nod along as Carla dishes out a list of controversial topics. The nodding, however, abruptly stops as she announces the last one, "Or society not even acknowledging the possibility that the Earth might not be round."

My heart sinks. There it is. She's a Flat Earther.

Bye-bye, true love.

Just to make sure, before I give up on her right away, I say, "You believe the Earth is flat?"

"Yeah, a round Earth makes some other phenomena unexplainable."

At this point, it's a mere fascination that prompts me to explore the topic. "Yeah, like what?"

"Railways, for example. The tracks run for miles across this country, and they're always flat. I mean, New York to LA, that supposed curvature should've come in at some point but, no. If the world was a globe curving eight inches per mile, the railways should be curved arcs, not flat lines. Or consider airplanes: if the Earth was a sphere 25,000 miles in diameter, pilots would have to constantly adjust their altitude to follow the slope, dipping the nose of the plane down, or they'd be flying straight into outer space. And yet, they fly straight."

"Well, no," I say. "Because gravity does the adjusting for them; it keeps the plane sort of on an orbit around the Earth."

"Oh, please, don't get me started on gravity."

Okay, this I *have* to hear. "Why not?"

"Because *'gravity'* is an obscure force supposedly strong enough to hold entire buildings, people, even the atmosphere, stuck to the surface of a rapidly spinning ball, but it's sufficiently weak enough to allow bugs, birds, and even planes to fly and travel in any direction. Don't you find that contradictory?"

"Um, if I remember correctly, gravity is a function of the weight of an object or the mass, I can't recall which. Physics was never my strong suit in school. Anyway, a bug doesn't weigh much, making its gravitational pull weak. It's why bird's bones are hollow, so they don't carry too much deadweight."

"Yeah? How do you explain the oceans, then? If gravity could curve and hold in place such massive expanses of water, how could fish ever swim through such forcefully held water?"

"I don't know. I'm not a scientist."

"See? A round Earth is counterintuitive. A much simpler explanation would be that the Earth is a flat expanse with no gravity."

"Do you really believe that?"

"Why not? You don't believe it only because you've been indoctrinated to think differently. But if you stopped for a second to question the scientific dogmas that have been force-fed to you since childhood, maybe you'd see there are other possible explanations."

"Like the Earth being flat." I laugh. "Sorry, I don't see that as an actual possibility."

Carla's face contracts into an indignant grimace, and she gets up, throwing her napkin on the table. "Oh my gosh, you're another fanatical of the"—she makes air quotes—"common sense club." She throws two twenty-dollar bills on top of her discarded napkin and adds, "I'm sorry, this isn't working out for me."

As she storms out of the restaurant, I can only think, *well at least this one paid for her half of the meal.*

* * *

This time, I don't tell Garrett about my date debacle. The last

155

thing I need is for Medusa to find out. Speaking of which…Vivian is unusually AWOL for the first two days of the following week. I have to wait until Tuesday night to bump into her as we're both leaving the office—and she positively knocks the breath out of me.

I've seen her dressed casually before. First, at Garrett and Leslie's engagement party, then for the date with the windbag. But tonight's outfit is a TKO! She's wrapped in a tight black dress that clings to her body like sin and lets me see every curve and plane. Her hair is loose over one shoulder, all glossy and wavy. And the shoes… How many stilettos does she own?

I enter the elevator after her, the familiar scent of vanilla and patchouli hitting my nostrils stronger than usual, as if she'd just sprayed herself.

In the most casual tone I can muster, I ask, "Out on a date?"

"Uh-huh."

"Isn't the agency's policy to set dates on the weekends?"

If I have to skip all the Knicks games to meet strange women, why does she get to go out on a random Tuesday night?

"For *first* dates, sure." Vivian flashes me a smug little smirk. "But since this is a second date, we can meet up whenever we like."

Second date? The announcement stings, and for a reason tragically unrelated to my professional housing situation.

"So, you've met The One?" I ask, nervous, needing more information. "Should I start packing boxes?"

"It's early days still. But Roger is a wonderful man."

Roger. What kind of name is that? Fit for a rabbit at best.

"Our first date was last Saturday," Vivian continues. "And we didn't want to wait two weeks to meet again. This weekend I would've been too worried about Tegan and her visit to her father, so we said, what the heck, why not go sooner?"

"Is he a good kisser?"

I swear, I have no idea what in the hell prompted me to ask that question.

"I'd imagine so." Vivian shrugs. "I'm probably going to find out tonight."

"That's a no, then. If he didn't kiss you after a great first date, he must be a lousy kisser. Wanted to put off the inevitable."

"Or maybe he's just a gentleman."

"Nah, I put my money on lousy kisser."

"You're insufferable. And anyway, I bet Roger is a better kisser than you."

"Yeah?"

The elevator has almost reached the lobby, and in ten seconds she's going to walk out and go on her wonderful date with Roger not the Rabbit, and kiss him on the way home, and I already hate this random stranger.

Before I can change my mind, I place a hand on her waist to draw her close, cup her cheek, and press my lips to hers. At first, she's rigid in my arms, but soon one of her hands shuffles up my chest while the other grips the hair at my nape, trying to pull me closer to her. Impossible; our bodies are already fused.

The kiss deepens and becomes more heated. I'm about to move my hands to much riskier areas when the elevator doors ding open and a startled "Oh!" makes us pull apart.

In the lobby, the tall, handsome man who runs the online magazine on our floor is staring at us with a shocked expression, which quickly turns into a wicked smile. "Please, don't stop on my account," he says in a posh British accent.

Vivian blushes tomato red, straightens her dress—which has ridden up her thighs, uncovering more delicious skin—and marches out of the elevator. "Don't worry," she snaps. "We were done. Good evening."

I follow her into the hall, and she waits until the man has left before pointing an accusing finger at me. "What did you do that for?"

"You weren't exactly an innocent bystander," I note.

"It was a spontaneous reaction, nothing more."

"Well, I'm glad I could bring out your basic instincts. Anyway," I shrug, acting a thousand shades cooler than I feel. "You bet me Roger is a better kisser than I am, how were you going to decide who wins otherwise?"

Her eyes narrow. "I'm going on my date now, and I will have fun and not think about you and your stupid bets."

She walks away, and the way her behind is swaying in that dress and those shoes sure doesn't help me get my head back on straight.

Yeah, go on your date, kiss Roger, I don't care.

On impulse, I take my phone out on the off chance that the *Listen to Your Heart* offices are still open.

Jennifer picks up on the second ring. "This is Jennifer, a *Listen to Your Heart* Dating Specialist. How may I help you?"

"Hello, this is Lucas Keller."

"Dr. Keller, good evening. What can I do for you?"

"I was wondering if you could find me another date for

this week. I'm busy on the weekend, but Thursday night would work great."

A brief pause. "What happened to *'I need a break from meeting new people'?*"

After the Flat Earther, I'd told her I needed to hit the brakes for a while.

"I've changed my mind," I say.

"Any particular reason?"

"No," I lie.

"Okay, Dr. Keller, I'll see what I can do and let you know."

"Fantastic."

I hang up and, before I make any more foolish decisions, I take a long, cooling walk home.

Twenty-one

Vivian

My lips are burning. My chest is burning. My core is burning. Every cell in my body is aflame.

I flee my office building and hail the first cab I see to get uptown.

Inside the car, I sit in the back, nervously biting on a nail while trying not to ruin the polish. I won't have that horrible man spoil the night for me.

So we made out in the elevator. Whatever. No big deal. I won't think about it.

I. Will. Not.

But no matter how hard I try to ignore what happened, the heat of that kiss doesn't leave me alone. Shrek did it on purpose. He wanted to ruin my date with Roger.

Why?

Probably to keep his stupid office. He's a selfish bastard.

Yeah, an evil little voice whispers in my ear, *because it's notorious for selfish bastards to spend their weekends driving someone else's kid to Boston so they can meet their father.*

Selfish or not, he's still a bastard.

The cab pulls up in front of the restaurant. I pay the driver and step on the curb, pulling the hem of my skirt down. Time to meet Roger. We're going to share a wonderful dinner and, at the end of the night, he's going to kiss me so passionately he'll make Lucas' pathetic little smooch pale in comparison.

Roger would have to be a pretty stunning kisser to one-

up Lucas, the same evil voice comments.

Oh, shut up.

Inside the restaurant, the hostess informs me I'm the first to arrive, and leads me to a table set for three.

"I'm sorry," I say. "There must be a mistake; I should be at a table for two."

The hostess checks her folder. "Is the reservation under Chapman?"

"Yes," I confirm.

"Then I have a reservation at 7:30 for three."

"Never mind," I say, and sit down.

The person who took the reservation must've written down the wrong number, but it's no big deal. They can clear the extra set of plates when Roger arrives. Tall, blond, with warm brown eyes, he's an architect and exactly the kind of man I should date: gentle, charming, polite, doesn't yell at strangers, and I'm sure he's never ambush-kissed anyone in his entire life.

Roger arrives a few minutes later, and I stand up to greet him. We hug. My nostrils fill with his scent, and I can't help but think the smell is wrong. Nothing foul, just the wrong scent.

And what would be the right *scent?* that same pestering voice asks.

Sandalwood and pine trees, I reply automatically, thinking of Lucas' cologne.

Oh, heck no. See? This is what he wanted: to get inside my head.

I will not think about Shrek or the way he kisses or smells. I. Will. Not.

Whatever you need to tell yourself, the pesky voice taunts.

As Roger and I pull apart, I show him our table, saying, "The restaurant must've gotten your reservation wrong; they gave us a table for three."

"Oh, no, that's right," he says, nonchalant. "There's someone I want you to meet."

For the first time, I notice a short woman in her middle fifties/early sixties lurking behind Roger. She's dressed in a conservative pastel pink tweed suit. On a *Project Runway* episode, the judges would describe her outfit as *matronly*. And that's exactly how she looks with her pearl earrings and necklace, heavy makeup, and chin-length, red curls so thoroughly hair-sprayed they don't move when she does.

Roger steps aside and makes the introduction. "Vivian, I wanted you to meet my mother, Ursula Chapman. Mom, this is Vivian."

I shake the woman's hand, and while she sits at our table, I whisper in Roger's ear, "You brought your *mother* to our second date?"

"Yeah," he replies, not even trying to keep his tone low. "I told you I valued my mom's opinion."

Um, not exactly. On our previous date, I mentioned my recent troubles with Tegan and school, and he said kids should always listen to their mothers. From that deceivingly innocent comment, I didn't imagine that, to him, the concept also applied to adults well past thirty.

Still standing and whispering, I ask, "And why is your mother joining us, exactly?"

Roger grabs my hands. "Vivian, I had a wonderful time with you on our first date, but before things can move forward in our relationship, I need to know we're compatible. I mean, what if we kept dating, and then Mom

162

didn't approve of you?"

What, indeed, I comment silently in my head, having a Charlotte on *Sex and the City* moment.

Roger must misinterpret the look on my face, because he adds, "Don't worry, I'm sure you'll pass the test with flying colors."

I inwardly scoff. Pity you just failed on all counts, Roger dear.

And I'm in for one miserable dinner—no Lucas to distract me this time.

As I sit down with a tight smile, I make two terrifying realizations. First, I went on a date with the new Norman Bates, and enjoyed myself so much I'd agreed to a rematch. And second, I'm inexplicably relieved things won't work out with Roger.

Why?

I will not think about that kiss.

Twenty-two

Lucas

I didn't rest well last night. It took me hours to fall asleep, tossing and turning in bed, tormented by images of Vivian on her stupid date. And when I finally passed out, she invaded my dreams, making my slumber none the more restoring. She truly put a spell on me.

By morning, I'm so tired I don't hear the alarm go off, and am only waking up now because Max, my rescue Jack Russell terrier, is gently licking my cheek.

My eyes fly open, and I roll over to check the bedside clock. *Whoops, I'm an hour late for his usual bathroom run.*

I scratch him behind the ears, saying, "Sorry, buddy, give me just a minute and we'll be out."

No time for a run, but I still have to walk Max.

As if sensing I could use a bit of male solidarity, Max gives me another small lick and drops his muzzle on my shoulder, whining.

"Thank you, buddy, but no, nothing you can do. I need to sort this out myself."

As the day progresses, my mental status doesn't improve. I spend the first hour at the office tensely listening for any sound outside and relax and tense simultaneously when I finally hear the click-clack of Vivian's heels on the landing. Is that the walk of a woman coming back from a wonderful date, or from a lousy kisser? I'm no Louboutin whisperer, so I've no way of telling.

The need to know what happened last night with Roger

keeps haunting me so much that, at lunch, I call Garrett and ask him if he's in the mood for a drink after work. If anyone can give me the inside scoop, it's him.

***

We meet at the Full Shilling as always and order beers at the bar. I spend the first twenty minutes making casual chit-chat so as not to appear too suspicious: how are things at work, have you guys set a date for the wedding, is Leslie driving you crazy with the planning, yadda, yadda, yadda...

When Garrett asks me how the new office is, I jump at the opportunity to introduce the topic that I came here to discuss.

"It's great," I say. "If I manage to keep the lease, that is."

Garrett raises an eyebrow. "Didn't you sign a one-year contract?"

"Yeah, but I don't know if Leslie told you... I also made a bet."

My friend smiles. "I might've heard something. Any luck with the agency so far?"

"My last date was with a Flat Earther," I say.

"Oh." Garrett laughs wholeheartedly. "You didn't tell me about that one."

"No, because you would've spilled everything to Leslie and, by transitive property, Vivian."

"Man, I don't have secrets with my fiancée. And it's not my fault women talk."

"To that effect, did you hear anything about Vivian's date last night?"

Garrett studies me for a few long seconds, before saying, "Turned out he was a real creep. The dude brought his mother along to *vet* Vivian."

Oh, I'd pay to see how that played out. Tension releases in my shoulders, and I let out a long breath. The world is a better place now.

"You seem relieved, man," Garrett says.

"Yeah." I shrug, trying to keep my attitude casual. "Because of the bet."

"Of course," Garrett says. *"The bet."*

Is he being sarcastic?

"Yeah, I'd like to keep my office. Better even, I want the corner one."

"So your curiosity has nothing to do with Vivian, the woman?"

"No, not at all."

"And you still don't like her?"

"Absolutely not."

Garrett raises that mocking eyebrow again. "Is that why you kissed her?" he asks, then takes another sip of beer.

Oh, for crying out loud, can't a man have any privacy?

He sees my expression and laughs. "Sorry, buddy. Like I said, women talk. Last night, Lee almost broke her neck running to tell me the news the moment she got off the phone with Vivian." He stares me down. "Are you *sure* there's nothing else going on?"

"Nothing," I say, adamant. "I don't know what possessed me last night, but I don't like her. Besides, I'm going on a date tomorrow night with another woman, possibly my future wife."

Jennifer called me earlier, announcing she'd managed to arrange a last-minute match for me.

"Okay, okay." Garrett raises his hands defensively. "I'm

just saying that if you did like her, there'd be nothing wrong with that. Vivian is a wonderful person. She's beautiful, fun, kind..."

In my head, I continue the list of her qualities, *and stubborn, and impossible to deal with, and the best kiss I've ever had, and—No wait, forget that last one!*

"She'd be a real steal," Garrett continues. "And Lee and I always thought you guys would make a perfect match."

Yeah, I comment in my head, *when hell freezes over.*

Despite my cocky denials, Garrett's words stay with me all the next day, and are still there, ringing in the background, as I enter the speakeasy-turned-restaurant I picked for my date with a Miss di Mauro.

After a few minutes seated at the table, I'm joined by a beautiful Indian woman with jet-black hair, dark eyes, and light-brown skin. We make the usual introductions and share our real names; hers is Mira. This time, however, I take a different approach to the getting-to-know-you phase and jump straight to the punch. "Can I ask you three really weird questions without you judging me? I promise there's a good reason."

Mira looks at me, half-amused, half-curious. "Sure," she says. "Fire away."

"Are you a witch?"

"Err... No?"

"What does the word 'fellow' mean to you?"

"Like an associate professor or a researcher?"

I sigh in relief and prepare myself for the ultimate test. "And finally, do you believe the Earth is round?"

Mira frowns. "Obviously. Why?"

I tell her the tragic story of my three previous dates set up by the agency, and she finds it hilarious. We laugh, drink wine, and share a wonderful meal while the conversation flows. Mira is sensual, intelligent, charming... and yet. I can't explain why nothing is taking off in my chest, not even the smallest spark of excitement.

Mira must feel the same way because, when the bill arrives and I offer to pay, she takes a long sip of wine and stares at me for a long moment before saying, "This has been a great date, and normally I'd accept your offer to cover dinner and ask you to join me somewhere else for a nightcap..."

"But?"

"But..." Another pause. "Feels to me like your heart wasn't really in it tonight. You act like someone who's hung up on another woman. Did your friends or family force you to join a dating agency to get over your ex or something?"

For a split second, I think about Brenda. Am I still not over her? I shake the idea away; I haven't spared my ex a thought in I don't even remember how long. She's not the issue.

That's when the image of a woman in a red coat with killer heels and a heart-shaped mouth pops into my head.

No, I can't be... Not with her...

But I am, I so am. I haven't been able to push Vivian out of my mind since that first glimpse of pink lace, and definitely not after I had the brilliant idea of kissing her.

These, however, are dreadful realizations I don't want to deal with now. So I share with Mira only part of the truth.

"Best friend," I say. "Garrett had been nagging me to join for weeks, then the night of his engagement party he came at me with the hard sell, and I finally caved."

"Ah." Mira sighs. "Champagne toasts and diamond rings. This friend used the heavy artillery."

"I guess he did."

"About tonight." Mira grabs the bill's leather folder and puts in her credit card. "I suggest we split dinner and leave as friends?"

"Friends sounds great."

***

Outside the restaurant, I say goodnight to Mira with a friendly hug, put her in a cab, and skip a ride home in favor of a walk. I'm taking a lot of late-night strolls these days.

The temperature is mild for nine p.m. in early May, and New York really is the city that never sleeps. As I wander the streets, lost in thought, I encounter all sorts of people: college students out for a cheap drink, club-goers, the socialites, the Wall Street types, older folks like myself going home after dinner, the hipsters, the artists... The city has it all. But the multicolored crowds aren't enough to distract me; my thoughts keep going back to a certain Attorney in Heels.

Where is she now? At home with Tegan? What are they doing? How long before the agency will send her on a date with someone else? And what if the next dude isn't a creep who brings his mother to second dates?

Vivian is beautiful, smart, and fun in her own very annoying way. It won't be long before a man who's not a complete fool snatches her up. The idea makes me want to puke. But what can I do about it? I can't ask her out; she'd laugh in my face. She hates my guts. Maybe not hate-hate, but she's strongly prejudiced against me, and how can I blame her? I attacked her out of nowhere when we first met, and I haven't always been on my best behavior around her. But only because she pushes my buttons so quickly she trips my sanity.

Right. I need to dispel her misconceptions about me. Yes, and I know where to start.

I'm a man with a plan.

Twenty-three

Vivian

Friday morning, I exit the elevator on my floor with the same wariness of the past two days. I haven't seen Shrek since *The Accident* on Tuesday night, and I have no idea how to behave around him now.

My strategy is doomed to failure, of course, as no later than tomorrow Lucas will pick up Tegan and drive her to Boston, and there'll be no avoiding him. But the longer I can put that awkward meeting off, the better.

Careful to walk on tiptoes as to not make any noise with my heels, I cross the landing to my door and unlock it. Still on stealth mode, I move into the office and close the door with the softest click. The sound echoes impossibly loud in my ears.

I'm being paranoid. No way Shrek heard that.

But I haven't even made it to the desk when a double knock on the door makes me jump. With no early appointments on today's schedule, there's only one person who would drop by unannounced.

I dump my briefcase on the desk and wait for another heartbeat. Maybe, if I pretend not to be here, Shrek will go away.

"I know you're in there," Lucas' voice calls from the other side.

He's so pretentious. I really can't stand him.

I take a deep breath, fuel my inner rage, and throw the door open. "What?" I say witheringly.

I was aiming for cold and haughty, but, gosh, does he have to look that good every single morning? Does he never get a bad hair day? Freshly shaven, in one of his usual impeccable suits, and with his smoldering blue eyes, he takes my breath away, melting all my coolness. His sandalwood scent finishes the work, destroying the last of my safeguards.

Unaware of the effect he's having on me, Lucas raises a pink paper bag, saying, "I come in peace and bearing donuts. We need to sit down and have a conversation."

My mouth waters a little, and I'm not sure if it's because of the donuts or thanks to the thought of sitting on top of Lucas—I mean, sitting *down with* Lucas. No one is sitting on top of anyone. Not in my office. And just like that, an image invades my mind: Lucas carrying me to the desk, clearing off the clutter with a sweep of his arm, and placing me on the hard, flat surface to kiss me until we're both breathless and dizzy.

Lucas' voice brings me back to the present. "Vivian?"

The way my name rolls off his tongue makes me shiver. I'm going insane. It's the only possible explanation.

Fighting to cool my spirit and tone, I ask, "Is it really necessary?"

"Yes." Lucas pushes past me, uninvited, into my office.

He lays a paper napkin on my side of the desk and places a perfectly glazed pink donut on top. Then he sits on one of the clients' chairs and bites with gusto on another equally pretty donut.

And never in my life would I have imagined being jealous of a pastry.

Without much of a choice, I sit at the desk, eyeing the fried treat suspiciously. A single bite would be enough to sell my soul to the devil, I'm certain. But, honestly, the glaze looks delicious—as does the devil—so I give in and relish the sugar rush. Then, since the anxiety is killing me—is he here to talk about the kiss?—I ask, "What is it you wanted to discuss?"

Lucas is sitting with an ankle resting on his knee as if he owns the place.

"Us," he says nonchalantly.

A simple word that causes a void to form in my stomach.

"What about *us?*" I ask. I won't mention the kiss unless he does.

Lucas uncrosses his legs. "We started on the wrong foot a month ago. Mostly my fault, I'll admit that." He gives me a cheeky smile that puts a warm fuzz in my belly. "Even if you did cut in front of me at the train station, and stole the last donut at Starbucks, and snatched the corner office of my dreams from under my nose all in less than an hour—"

"If you're still going on about—"

Lucas raises his hands placatingly. "I'm not. I just wanted to contextualize my reaction of that day. I was stressed about the office situation, and you'd rubbed my feathers the wrong way, so I snapped. Not something I do often, for the record. And I should've apologized a long time ago, but then the moving truck incident happened, and the bet, and things kept escalating for no reason. And I'm tired of it. I'm tired of being at odds with you all the time. So I came here this morning to say sorry, and to ask if we can leave the sworn enemies phase behind us and please be friends."

Friends?

I'm not sure why, but the word irks me to no end. Maybe because Dr. Smooch is conveniently glossing over the fact that, not two days ago, he was eating my face in the elevator. Are we really going to pretend that kiss never happened?

"Why apologize now?" I ask.

"Tomorrow is an important day. I want you to trust me before I bring Tegan to meet her father."

If I were a braver woman, I'd ask him if that's the only reason for the ceasefire. But I'm not, so I go along with the let's-pretend-our-tongues-were-never-in-each-other's-mouths flow.

I finish my second, unplanned breakfast and lick my fingers, not missing the way Lucas' eyes follow my every movement. "And was the donut a bribe?"

He smiles. "Did it work?"

I clean my hands with a paper napkin and lean my elbows on the desk. "All right, Doctor." I extend my hand, saying, "Friends?"

"Friends."

We shake on it, his eyes bluer than ever.

The contact and the eye lock are too much, so I break both by grabbing some random documents from the desk and tapping them on the wooden surface as if I needed to tidy the stack. "If there's nothing else...? I have a busy morning."

Lucas scratches the back of his head. "Actually, I need to ask you a favor for tomorrow."

The man is driving my daughter to Boston; I can hardly refuse. "Sure, what is it?"

"My dog sitter isn't available tomorrow—she doesn't work weekends—and Max wouldn't enjoy the four-hour drive back and forth. Could you keep him for the day?" And before I can answer, he adds, "He's a good dog, I promise, and you'd only need to walk him twice and feed him."

"Yeah, no problem. Is Max a big dog?"

"No, a Jack Russell, hardly a heavyweight."

"And is he okay with cats?"

Lucas grimaces. "Eeeh, I'm not sure. But if you can't keep him, I can always ask Garrett."

"No," I say. "It's fine. I'll be happy to take Max."

"Great."

We both stand up, and I walk him to the door.

Lucas leans against the frame in an unfairly sexy pose, saying, "See you tomorrow."

I'm drawn in by some magnetic force and lean forward. But before I do something stupid, like press against him and kiss those sinfully full lips, I back off, coughing out, "Tomorrow."

Then I shut the door in his face.

Out of sight, out of mind.

***

The next morning, the doorbell rings at eight on the dot. Tegan has been up since the crack of dawn and promptly rushes to the front door to answer. She's greeted by a bout of barking, and I hear cooing sounds as she lavishes attention on Lucas' dog. They seem to get along.

Priscilla is not on the same page; she scurries down the hall and regards me accusingly.

"Don't worry, Prissy, it's only for today."

The cat glares at me, still indignant, and goes to hide in Tegan's room.

As I shuffle down the hall, I'm not nearly as presentable as I would've liked to be, but I overslept. So, I have no other choice than to go meet Lucas wearing an oversized sweater, leggings, and my hair down in a rat's nest mess. I check my reflection in the hall mirror and try to pull my hair up in a messy bun. But that looks even worse, so I let it back down, quickly combing my fingers through the tangled locks.

Oh, whatever. I turn the corner and briefly take in my daughter crouched on the floor patting a tiny dog, before I'm shocked by the sight of Lucas wearing dark-blue jeans and a gray V-neck. His eyes widen in return upon spotting me, and it kills me I've no idea what he's thinking.

"Wow," I say, "you do own casual clothes. I thought you were Neil Patrick Harris' secret twin and went to bed in pajama suits."

Lucas smiles, although I'm not sure he caught the *How I Met Your Mother* reference. "It's good to see you out of your lawyer uniform, too."

Excited by a new arrival, Max escapes Tegan's arms and rushes at my feet, jumping and barking.

I crouch to the floor. "And who's this little guy?" I scratch the dog behind the ears, and he tries to lick my face.

Lucas squats next to us. "Glad to see you two get along."

I swear, his eyes haven't always been this blue, nor his lips so full and inviting… I bite my lower lip and catch him watching me. The moment is interrupted when Tegan steps in, saying, "Are we good to go?"

We jump up, and Lucas hands me a small bag, saying, "Max's leash and food are inside. If he gives you any trouble, let me know."

"I'm sure he won't."

"All right," Lucas says. "We'd better go."

Sober now, I say, "Text me constant updates."

He nods.

I turn to Tegan, and my heart breaks a little. What will happen today?

I pull my daughter into a hug. "I love you, baby."

For once, she doesn't pull away with an indignant, *"Mom, I'm not a child anymore!"*

Tegan hugs me back just as tightly, saying, "I love you, too."

Holding Max in my arms so as not to let him run down the street, I watch them cross over to where Lucas has parked his black SUV. They get into the car and, in a heartbeat, they're gone.

To kill time, I spend the morning compulsively cleaning the house while staring at my watch every five seconds. A single text breaks the routine:

In Hartford, stopping for gas
and a bathroom break

It's not much, but at least Lucas is keeping me posted as promised.

Max has been following me around the house, sniffling at every corner, while Priscilla has kept to the safety of Tegan's room—the only place Max hasn't dared enter, as if an unspoken message has passed between the two pets.

I'm finishing scrubbing the bathtub when the cute dog bumps me with his muzzle. I sit back on my heels and find him staring up at me, head tilted, and a red leash between his jaws. The message couldn't be clearer.

I stare at my watch. It'll take Lucas and Tegan at least another hour to arrive in Cambridge, and their appointment isn't until two. We have plenty of time for a walk, and I could use the fresh air.

Outside, I head toward Whitman Park while Max stops to sniff at every tree and fire hydrant we pass on the way. Before we reach the park, I pause at a kiosk to buy a sandwich. The day is warm, so I sit on a bench in the sun and share bites of my lunch with Max. When I'm finished, I don't get up right away. Instead, I tilt my head up and enjoy the hot sun rays hitting my face. And, if not relaxed, at least I'm calm when my phone pings with a new incoming text.

> In Cambridge, we're finding a place to have lunch and then we're going to the university

Fifteen minutes later, another message arrives: a picture of Tegan biting on an oversized burger. She looks nervous but happy.

"Time to go home, buddy," I tell Max.

When the meeting takes place, I want to be at home with no distractions. It's an all-hands-on-deck situation, since I have no idea what the outcome will be. If Tegan needs me, even long distance, I want to be there.

Two o'clock comes and goes while I sit on the couch, mercilessly biting at the cuticles on my fingers and staring at the black TV screen with a lump in my throat. Max must sense I'm nervous, because he drops his muzzle on my thigh and stares up at me, worried.

That's when Pricilla comes out of her hiding hole. She throws one deadly glare at me and the dog usurping her space and narrows her eyes.

In response, Max lowers his ears and stares daggers at the cat in return. Prissy turns on her paws, even more indignant, regaling us with a view of her uptight behind as she goes back into hiding.

When I stare back at my phone after the short distraction, a new message has appeared on screen—a short, terrifying one.

> Tegan is going in now

How did I not hear the ping? I check the tones are on and put the ringer to max volume. Shortly afterward, another text comes in, announced by a sound this time.

> How are you holding up?

> > I'm sick to my stomach

> That good, uh?

> I know it's useless to say you shouldn't worry

> But really, don't worry

> Whatever is happening in there, Tegan will be the better for it afterward

She's strong, like you

And if words could help, Lucas' would have. Maybe they have, a little. Talking with Lucas is a nice diversion from staring at the black TV screen, so I make light of the exchange.

I'm a mom

It's part of the job description to worry

What about Max?

Is he being a good boy?

Lucas must be changing the subject to distract me, but why not play along?

He's been an angel all day

Max didn't try to eat your cat? I was worried he might

No, Priscilla went into hiding as soon as he set a paw in the house, so he didn't have a chance

> We're on the couch now
>
> Max's taking care of me with lots of cuddles

That's a lucky dog

Even through the anguish of the moment, his words make my heart skip a beat. I'm trying to come up with a cool reply when another text lights the screen.

Tegan is coming out now

She slammed the door

Going after her

What did her father say to induce such a strong reaction? That bastard. I knew he'd hurt her. It's all he's capable of doing. I should've never agreed to let them meet. I knew better.

I send Lucas a worried message:

> What's going on?

No answer.

> Lucas, please, I'm dying
> here

Still nothing.

I try to call him, but he doesn't pick up. After a few unbearably long minutes, a reply finally comes in.

> It didn't go well

"No kidding," I snap in frustration, and read the next text.

> I know as much as you, but
> Tegan is okay

> Or will be okay, soon

> She's agreed to let me buy
> her ice cream

> We're going to talk, and then
> I'll take her home to you

> Go easy on yourself, this is
> not on you, but him, and
> only him

> And, again, don't worry,
> Tegan is safe with me

I was already blaming myself for everything, when Lucas' texts force me to pause. Yeah, except for having had zero taste in men when I was a teen, I can't turn bad people into decent ones with the flip of a magic wand. We all have to deal with our choices, and I've come to terms with mine. It's killing me not to be there to comfort Tegan, but I'm also strangely relieved to know she's with Lucas. Despite our rocky relationship, he's the only man I've ever trusted with the wellbeing of my daughter. Weird, uh?

***

When they arrive home much later that evening, Tegan flies into my arms, hugging me tightly. I hold her, too, and we stay in this position for a few minutes.

Lucas is keeping a few steps back, waiting respectfully on the front porch. I mouth a "Thank you," at him over Tegan's shoulder. He nods.

Once Tegan lets me go, I invite Lucas in, but he refuses. "I'd better go. It's late, and you girls have a lot to talk about."

Upon hearing his favorite human's voice, Max comes rushing down the hall to greet Lucas.

I give Lucas the leash and thank him again. Tegan does the same, hugging him, and then both the dog and his owner are gone.

Tegan and I sit on the couch, and I don't know where to start. I have so many questions.

Probably sensing the house is finally free of canine invaders, Priscilla saunters through the living room and moves into the kitchen for her first meal of the day, while her lowered ears and scorned attitude ensure we understand how deeply offended she still is.

Well, Missy, today we all had to deal with unpleasant shit. Welcome to the club.

Unable to bear another minute of waiting, I ask Tegan, "Do you want to talk about what happened?"

Tegan turns the ring on her middle finger. "Actually, I'd like to hear your side of the story first. Can you tell me why you didn't want me to meet him?"

I tell her everything. That I fell in love with my professor, got pregnant, and that he blackmailed me into changing schools.

Tegan nods along, her eyes getting watery as she listens to the story. When I'm finished, we're both crying.

She hugs me again, saying, "I'm sorry, Mom."

"Don't be, honey, it wasn't your fault."

"No, I know, but whenever you said my father wasn't worth my pinky toe and I was better off without him, I thought you were exaggerating, that you were angry. But you were right. He's not worth our grief."

"Oh, baby, what happened today?"

"He denied everything. Claimed you were obsessed with him and must've invented the entire story. Then he added that he was sorry, he didn't know who my father was, but it absolutely wasn't him."

I've meant no one harm in my entire life, but that man is getting dangerously close.

"And how did you respond?" I ask, trying to keep calm, fighting the urge to rent a car and drive to Boston in the middle of the night to punch the bastard in the face.

"All I could think was that our eyes are the same color. It was freakish to stare at him; like looking in the mirror."

"Yes, you have the same eyes."

"Do you hate to see him in me?"

I push a lock of hair behind her ear. "No, sweetheart, I love everything about you. You're the only good thing that man ever gave me."

"I called him a liar," Tegan admits.

"How did he react to that?"

"He said the apple doesn't fall far from the tree, and that I was just as crazy as you, and then he threatened me. Told me never to apply to Harvard and that, if I did, he'd make sure I wouldn't get in."

Man, he's lucky he's two hundred miles away from me right now.

"I'm sorry he said those things, honey. But I promise you, if you want to go to Harvard, we'll find a way. Don't be scared."

"I'm not scared, Mom, I'm *angry*. He blackmailed you and threatened me. My father is a bully, and now he's in a position of even more power. What if we're not the only women he's mistreated?"

"What are you saying, baby?"

"I want you to go public with what he did. Even if what he did wasn't strictly illegal, it must've been unethical." The fire of injustice burns in Tegan's eyes as she talks. "I'm sure Harvard wouldn't keep such a scum person on their faculty, and I don't want him to ruin anyone else's life."

Lucas was right. Tegan is strong, independent, and empowered. And she's also right: her father has bullied his last victim.

Twenty-four

Lucas

Mid-session with a new couple, the Friedmans, my phone vibrates in my pocket. I discreetly check the screen, in case it's an emergency, and discover it's Jennifer from *Listen to Your Heart*. I let the call go unanswered. The last thing I need on a Monday morning after the tough weekend in Boston is to talk to my Dating Specialist. And since I've learned her tactics the hard way, before she can try my landline, I excuse myself and unhook the receiver on my desk.

"Sorry about that," I tell my patients as I sit back in my armchair. "Where were we?"

Today, I'm dealing with a distinguished couple in their late fifties, who have shown each other about as much warmth as two ice cubes so far.

Mr. Friedman replies first. "I was telling you how my wife betrayed me."

"I did no such thing," his wife snaps. "He's just sore because he lost his seat in the council."

"Yes, because I wasn't willing to sell my soul to get elected!"

I clear my throat. "Are you in politics?"

"We both used to sit on the Lackawanna City Council," Mrs. Friedman explains, "until last year when he wasn't reappointed."

"Because you conspired against me," the husband cuts in. "She sabotaged me to get a spot for her best friend."

The wife raises her chin, proud. "I did what I thought best

for the city."

Before Mr. Friedman can spill more venom, I raise my hands to calm their spirits. "Okay, okay, so you're having a very specific conflict related to this election. Is that when your conjugal problems started?"

The couple blinks at me, as if I'd just asked them to please dance on the couch naked.

I rephrase the question. "How long have you been having issues as a couple?"

The wife scoffs. "When *haven't* we had problems?"

"Why choose therapy now, then?"

Mrs. Friedman replies again, "He's a sore loser, and his constant whining has become unbearable."

I try a different angle. "Let's talk about other aspects of your relationship. How is your sex life?"

"Excellent." The husband surprises me with his answer, but then he adds, "I never take it home."

The wife doesn't even flinch.

I sigh and close the scratchpad I was taking notes on. I recognize a lost cause when I see one. "Mr. and Mrs. Friedman, I'm sorry, but my professional opinion is that you're past counseling as a couple." And I surprise even myself when, next, I add, "If you need a divorce lawyer, I can recommend a wonderful attorney. And you wouldn't even have to change buildings; Miss Hessington works just next door."

Once I've shown the Friedmans to the door, I sit at my desk and replace the landline receiver. Then I check my phone for messages. None. But there *are* three missed calls, all from *Listen to Your Heart*. Jennifer won't give up, and I'd rather rip the Band-Aid instead of spending the morning dreading her next attempt, so I call her back.

"Dr. Keller!" my Dating Specialist picks up on the first ring. "How great to hear from you. Sorry I wasn't able to reach out sooner, but the weekends are always a busy time. I wanted to collect your feedback on your date Thursday night. Did you enjoy your evening?"

"Yes," I reply truthfully.

"And did you feel you and Miss Di Mauro were compatible?"

Like always, she sticks to our aliases instead of real names.

"Yes, but—"

"How wonderful," Jennifer cuts me off in a wave of enthusiasm. "And if Miss Di Mauro also gives me positive feedback, would you be interested in a second date?"

"No."

"I beg your pardon?"

"I said I don't want a second date with Mira."

"But... why?"

"There was no spark."

"No spark," Jennifer repeats, and then takes a brief pause. Did I finally rock her boat?

Nuh-uh. Two seconds are enough for her to recover and get back on the warpath. "Okay, Dr. Keller, you're a tough nut to crack, but I don't give up easily. What if we tried something different for a change?"

"Different how?" I ask warily.

"Well, you're not hitting it off with the women best suited for you, so... How about we try matching you with someone completely wrong for you on paper? You know, try an 'opposites attract' strategy."

"Wouldn't that be a recipe for disaster?"

"Well, Dr. Keller, everything we've tried so far hasn't worked, so it's time to think outside the box. Or do you no longer want to find true love?"

Despite my better judgment, I agree with Jennifer's crazy idea. One more terrible date won't kill me, and at least I'll be able to ask for a refund afterward.

***

I let Vivian process what's happened with Tegan's father for a few more days before I press the topic again. In an ideal world she would've already reached out, but Vivian has been AWOL all week. For a lawyer, she sure doesn't like confrontations when it comes to her personal life. Her trust issues with men make a lot more sense now that I know about Tegan's father. But by Friday it really is past time we talked about this, so I show up at her office door bright and early, armed with more donuts and Vivian's favorite coffee order—vanilla latte, as kindly disclosed by Tegan.

She opens the door, taking me in alongside the box of donuts and coffee tray. "Why am I not surprised?" she asks, her lips parting in a smile.

Bun tighter than ever, she's wearing another one of her purplish suits. If I were meeting her for the first time, I'd still call the ensemble stern. But now I know what lacy secrets hide under those pencil skirts, and I can't stop thinking how good it'd feel to untie her hair and let it flow through my fingers like silk.

I'm still staring like an idiot when Vivian speaks again. "Are you doubling as a delivery boy, or did you have a reason to be here?"

And I must've gone mad, because I'm even starting to enjoy her banter.

"I'd like to talk about last weekend, and the donuts are to sweeten the pill a little. You have time?"

"Would it matter if I said no?"

"If you're not in the mood for donuts and a vanilla latte—skim milk, extra vanilla pump—I can come back later."

Vivian's eyes widen upon hearing the description of her favorite coffee blend, and her smile gets bigger. "Gosh, you're good at getting me to do things I don't want to do." She steps aside. "Come on in."

I wait for her to be properly caffeinated and sweetened before I ask, "How are you holding up?"

"That's not just a conversational interlude—you want a proper answer, right?"

"I'd like one, yes."

"Has Tegan said anything?"

I nod. "She's processing and recovering fast from the blow. But you're a big part of her world, and she can tell you're upset."

"I am," Vivian admits. "I'm furious that bastard disowned Tegan a second time and threatened her, but... Coming clean has lifted a huge weight off my chest. It's wonderful to no longer have secrets with my daughter, not to live with the constant fear of Tegan finding out what a jerk her father is. The worst has already happened, and now we can both move on." She pauses for a moment, turning the paper cup in her hands, and then raises her big, Bambi eyes on me. "And you were right, by the way. Sharing the truth brought us closer."

My lips curl. "I'm sorry, I must've heard wrong. Did you just say I was right?"

"Now, don't go getting a big head, Doctor, you're still an awful neighbor. But I have to admit you're a decent therapist."

"Oh, come on, would an awful neighbor bring you your favorite breakfast?"

"I thought you were acting in counselor capacity."

"And as a friend. If you're still okay with being friends, that is."

She looks startled. "You're worried about me?"

"Is that okay?"

"I suppose…"

We hold stares for a long time, as if we're playing a game of whoever-drops-their-gaze-first loses. But I'm not interested in competing, so, with the excuse of taking another donut out of the box, I break the eye contact. And Vivian breaks the silence.

"Can I ask you something?"

"Sure."

"Did Tegan tell you about her plan? To denounce her father, and possibly get him fired?"

I nod.

"What do you make of it?" she presses. "Is it an act of pointless revenge, or does it have merit?"

"What do *you* think?"

"Is answering questions with other questions part of your shrinking voodoo, Doc?"

"Sorry, I can't share my secret juju."

Vivian rolls her eyes but answers my question all the same. "I'm torn. Tegan's right when she says I should've reported her father years ago, and that if he's been treating other women the same, he needs to be stopped…"

"But?"

"But I'm also worried she's just seeking revenge out of spite. He rejected her, and she's lashing out. And I'm not sure a tit-for-tat approach is healthy."

I consider for a moment. "I don't think Tegan is being petty. Yeah, she's mourning the fantasy of a joyful reunion with her long-lost father, but Tegan went to the meet with no preconceptions—good or bad. She formed her judgment all on her own—and what she saw was a predator in a position of authority who needs to be stopped. I believe she's being objective. With no previous relationship factoring into her judgment, he doesn't hold any power on her..."

"Contrary to me, you mean?"

"We can't help it. Whenever we love someone, we give that person power over us, and that influence can linger for a long time even after the love is gone."

"You know what? I'm tired of being kept under his thumb. I don't want to fear him anymore. Tegan is right; we should fight back."

Gosh, when Miss Attorney gets this passionate, she's so beautiful... I wonder how she looks when she's making love—

"Did I say something wrong?" Vivian's voice cuts into my X-rated fantasy.

I cough. "Err... no. Why?"

"You have a weird expression." Her eyes narrow. "Are you blushing?"

"No, of course not." I tug my finger at my shirt collar. "It's just boiling in here. Aren't you hot?"

She shrugs. "Seems perfectly fine to me."

"Well, I don't want to steal any more of your time." I get

up, afraid of what I might say or *think* next. "I should go."

Vivian walks me to the door and holds it open for me, but before I can leave, she stops me, her hand gently grabbing my arm.

"Thank you for Saturday," she says. "And for everything else."

Her eyes are big and warm... and her mouth is so close. If I leaned down just a few inches, I could kiss her again.

Suddenly, I don't want to go anymore. I hesitate on the threshold, saying, "I'm glad I could help you and Tegan. It's great to make a difference in someone's life." Then I scramble for something else to say, blabbing the first thing that pops into my head. "By the way, thank you for sending Mrs. Elkins to me. I was surprised the referral came from you."

Vivian waves me off. "Oh, please, you did the same with the Friedmans. And besides, it was obvious Jade was still in love with her husband. I would never suggest a divorce when it's not warranted."

"You did with the Thomases."

"I hadn't pinned them down as the second chance type of couple. It took your..."

She flaps her hands, searching for the right word, so I offer, "Shrinking voodoo?"

"Yep, that, to patch them up."

Vivian watches me, and I frantically search for the next thing to say. Nothing comes, so she speaks again. "Well, anyway, at least the week is almost over. I've had enough of work."

And she's given me the perfect conversational hook. "I hope you're doing something less stressful this weekend."

"Oh, yes. I have a date on Saturday."

My good mood evaporates.

"Yeah," I mutter. "I have one of those as well."

I really don't want to discuss her going on dates with other men, so I take a step back, putting some distance between us.

"I need to go now and get my thoughts in order before my next clients arrive in twenty minutes."

Beating a hasty retreat, I cross the hall to my door. Vivian lingers on the threshold, leaning with a shoulder on her doorframe.

"Good luck on your date," she calls after me. "I hope she isn't a witch this time."

I unlock the door and pause for a second before getting in, locking eyes with Vivian. "And I hope he won't bring his mother."

I wink, and stare in satisfaction at Vivian's jaw as it drops in outrage. Before all hell can break loose, I seek refuge in the safety of my office.

Twenty-five

Vivian

As I get ready for dinner in the city Saturday night, I'm not as enthusiastic as I should be. Maybe because, so far, the agency has only set me up with losers. I've complained, but, according to Barbara, my Dating Specialist, the next great American novelist was on his first spin and hadn't been vetted yet. And with Roger, she told me I was the only woman to ever be approved for a second date, so she had no way of knowing he'd bring his mother along.

When Barbara and I got off the phone, I didn't know if I should be flattered or scared to death that mama's-boy liked me so much.

Anyway, my dating specialist has assured me she's stepped up her game, and that my date tonight should leave me breathless. Barbara has described my mystery man as handsome and a real catch. So, why can't I summon some excitement?

I wonder how Lucas feels. From what Lee has told me, his dates have been even worse than mine—not to mention the dreadful one I witnessed firsthand. The agency must've found a pretty special woman for him, too, tonight if they hope to keep their reputation and our business.

A little ball of acid spreads in my stomach. Oh, I must already be hungry. Weird, because I ate a substantial lunch with Tegan today, to celebrate putting her father behind us once and for all. Yesterday, after speaking with Lucas, I drafted two affidavits. The first, detailing what happened to me as a student all those years ago. And the other, reporting Tegan's testimony of last weekend. This morning we signed and posted them, and by now, the envelopes should be on their way to Boston. And if that pig ever tries any legal action for defamation, a simple DNA test would bulletproof our defense.

Anyway, this date I'm going on... Even if I don't feel the romantic vibes yet, I'm still dressing for the part. Okay, I'm not going through the motions like I did for brunch with Mr. Tolstoy—no one-hour makeup tutorials, curly irons, or fancy new dresses. But the midi dress I'm wearing is cute and sexy in a silly, carefree way with its floral print. I have makeup on, high heels, and my hair is loose on my shoulders. Blow drying got me natural, shiny waves, and if that's not good enough for my mystery man, well, he can take a hike for all I care.

I exit the house together with Tegan—she's going to the movies with her best friend, Jesse. Under the scrutiny of Priscilla, who's watching us from one of the downstairs windows, we kiss goodbye on the front steps.

Tegan is walking to her friend's house, so she goes first while I wait for my cab to arrive. When the car screeches to a halt next to me only a few minutes later, I open the rear door and, before getting in, wave to Priscilla, who glares at me and then disappears into the living room to do who knows what now that she has the house all to herself.

Twenty minutes later, the taxi stops in front of La Masseria, a nice Italian restaurant in Midtown.

I pay the driver with my credit card and get out of the cab. Inside the restaurant, I give my date's alias to the hostess.

"Ewing for two at eight-thirty," the hostess repeats. "Mr.

Ewing hasn't arrived yet, but I can show you to your table."

The young woman guides me to a table by the window— *set for two, yay.* I sit, staring at the city lights outside.

Let's hope this won't be another half an hour's wait for the next great American anything.

Twenty-six

Lucas

I hate being late, even if only by ten minutes. Unfortunately, traffic was terrible, and I've yet to develop the ability to move cars with my mind. When my taxi pulls up in front of the restaurant I picked for my date tonight, I fish two twenty-dollar bills out of my wallet and hand them to the driver, saying, "Keep the change."

I'm majorly over-tipping, but I don't have time to wait for a credit card transaction. I might not have big expectations for tonight, but the poor Miss Pocahontas doesn't deserve to be left waiting.

Inside the restaurant, I give the hostess my alias.

"Oh, yes, Mr. Ewing, your date has already arrived," she informs me, and beckons me to follow her.

We head to a corner table near the window—as per my request—where a brunette is sitting with her back to me while she looks out to the street, giving me an unobstructed view of her profile.

Her nose is narrow and straight, her eyes big and brown, and I would recognize that heart-shaped mouth in a heartbeat.

I should know; I was kissing those lips not ten days ago.

My pulse races, and I can't help the huge smile that tears at my cheeks.

"Here's your table, Mr. Ewing," the hostess says. "A server will be with you soon."

The hostess is already turning to go welcome some other

guests when my date looks up.

And I love that I had a few seconds' advantage on her. Vivian's eyes widen, while her jaw positively drops.

I greet her with a charming, "Good evening, Miss Pocahontas. I hope you haven't been waiting too long?"

Her shock is quickly replaced with suspicion. "What are you doing here?" she demands.

"I believe I'm your date for the night."

"There must be a mistake."

Taking a risk, I lean down and kiss her on the cheek, then quickly retreat to my half of the table before she can protest. "You're right," I say, "it might be a mistake. I'm here to meet Miss Pocahontas. Ever heard of her?"

Vivian narrows her eyes. "So you're Mr. Ewing?"

"That's right." I shrug. "Some algorithm somewhere must've decided we're a match."

I sure won't tell her my dating specialist sent me on an "outside the box opposites attract" kind of date. Makes me wonder how Vivian answered her questionnaire. Wish I could get my hands on a copy.

"And about time," I continue, taking a seat. "I was convinced this whole dating agency thing had been a total rip-off. I agreed to a date with Miss Pocahontas only to make sure they'd give me a refund."

"So all I am to you is a refund?" Vivian snaps, focusing on the one negative thing I said and taking it out of context. "If that's the case, we can get up right now and, when the agency calls on Monday, I can let them know what an ass—"

"Calm down." I raise my hands in an attempt to stop the tirade. "I said that I went out with *Miss Pocahontas* to get a refund. But right now, I'd be happy if the agency charged me double because there's no other place I'd rather be than on a date with *you,* Vivian Hessington the Divorce Lawyer."

A little smile tugs at her lips. "Is that what you call me inside your head?"

"Among other things."

"Such as?"

No point in dragging my feet. If Vivian wants to know, she'll get it out of me eventually. So, I confess, "I might have referred to you as The Wicked Witch of the West Office..."

Her mouth contracts in the cutest outraged O shape for a second, but then the smile is back, and she says, "Fair enough."

Her attitude throws me, until my brain connects the dots. "What names have *you* been calling me inside your head?"

Vivian shrugs. "Shrink Shrek."

"Shrek? Why?"

Her smile turns evil. "You share the same charming temper."

"You mean, a little grumpy at first, but then a real darling once you get to know us?"

Vivian stares at me. "Something like that." Then she bursts out laughing. "Funny how we've been characterizing each other like green monsters."

"Glad we're past that." I clear my throat. "Now that we've clarified why I'm here... May I ask why you've decided to stay?"

"I never said I had."

"You're still sitting."

"I told you, you're great at making me do things I don't want to do."

"Just to be clear, you don't want to be on a date with me? Because if I remember correctly, it wasn't just me in that elevator."

She blushes. Then, looking at me with an intense light in her eyes, she says, "No, it wasn't."

"Great," I say, placing my napkin on my legs. "So, can we please stop pretending we don't like each other and have dinner?"

"Sounds like a good plan."

Twenty-seven

Vivian

Outside the restaurant, Lucas insists on sharing a cab ride home, even if we don't live anywhere near each other. Still, I agree.

Dinner was fantastic, and I'm not just talking about the upscale Italian food. When the meal ends, I'm not ready for our date to be over. Now that I've let some of my walls down, I can finally admit that I like Lucas. He's funny, charming, handsome, a stellar kisser...

Oh, who am I kidding? My barriers are lowered all the way, have been for a while.

In the back of the cab on the ride home, we don't talk. But my heart beats faster and faster the closer we get to my house.

And when the taxi finally stops on my street, the jitters worsen.

I offer to cover the ride, but Lucas refuses, just like he did when I tried to pay my half of the bill at the restaurant. Letting the man pay might be old-fashioned, but I'm okay accepting a little gallantry. Especially if it's coming from him.

Lucas walks me to the front steps, where I stop to face him.

"You know I can't invite you in. Tegan is home."

His smile is positively wicked. "Why on Earth couldn't I come in while your daughter's home? Unless..." His eyes widen comically large. "Miss Hessington, don't tell me you were thinking of doing naughty, *naughty* things to me."

My knees melt at the mere mention of *naughty things*. I haven't been with a man in forever, and I'm sure Lucas would make the wait worthwhile.

Now he takes a step closer, and with his finger traces the contour of my collarbone. His exploration continues along my shoulder and over to my bra strip, which he tugs into view—bright magenta lace. What can I say? I have a thing for fancy lingerie.

"What—what are you doing?" I stammer.

Eyes all dark and intense, Lucas says, "Just testing a theory."

Lucas' hand lets go of my bra strap and rises in a slow caress to cup my cheek.

"And now what are you doing?"

"I'm kissing you, like any sane man would at the end of a great date."

Lucas' mouth is on mine in a heartbeat, leaving me no time to reply. I don't even try to pretend I'm not all-in for the kissing. I dive right in, sinking my fingers into his soft hair and pressing my body to his.

Without the ticking clock of an elevator ride, I have no idea how long the kiss lasts. But it's almost definitely an indecent amount of time. And I'm a little ashamed to admit that, when Lucas finally pulls back, I want more. *So* much more.

From the way he's looking at me, it's clear we're on the same page.

Why didn't we go to *his* house?

"Would it be too soon to ask you on a second date?" Lucas asks.

I smile. "No."

"How about tomorrow? Or is that too soon?"

"It's not, but... Sorry, this week has been a nightmare for me." I put my hands forward. "It's not an excuse; I really have a ton of work to do. I should hire a paralegal to help me out, but I'm the worst at delegating. Even for the smallest things."

"Relax," Lucas says, unperturbed. "I've waited this long. I can wait for another week."

"What do you mean, you've waited this long?"

"Well, in case you haven't noticed, I've been trying to woo you for a while now."

"Really? How?" And then something clicks in my brain. "Is that what the donuts were about? I thought the sweets were a professional courtesy."

"None of my other clients get a hand-delivery of their favorite breakfast, I can assure you."

I can't stop the huge, silly smile that parts my lips. "Bribery and attempted corruption of an attorney-at-law! You've been terrible, Dr. Keller."

"Is that a 'no' to more donuts and vanilla lattes?"

"Well, a girl has to eat..."

"Especially breakfast," Lucas adds. "It's the most important meal of the day."

"Right, I'm basically forced to say yes. But can we make it an early breakfast? I'm swamped with casework all week."

"Deal," Lucas says. He leans in closer and whispers, "Good night, Vivian," before he kisses me again.

***

I expect the house to be silent when I get in, and for Tegan to be already in bed. Instead, she's waiting for me behind the entrance door, barely leaving me enough room to step into the hall before she barrels into me.

"Was that Luke?" she asks, hopping from foot to foot with her hands joined in front of her chest. "Were you kissing him?"

"What are you doing still up?"

"Don't change the subject! You were totally kissing Luke. But how? Weren't you supposed to be on a blind date?"

"I was, honey, only the agency paired me with Lucas."

"Really?" She claps. "How wonderful! So, you like Luke now? Didn't you hate him?"

I kick off my heels and massage my ankles. "I never said I *hated* him."

"Oh, Mom, it doesn't matter." Tegan wraps her arms around my waist. "I'm just glad it's Luke."

"Yeah," I say, hugging her back.

"Luke would be the best stepfather," she says idly, a faraway look in her eyes.

I keep holding my daughter, wondering which one of us is developing the biggest expectations about this relationship. I'm afraid we might be two goners. And I should be cautious before I let my feelings roam wild… but, for once, I don't want to be cautious. I want to enjoy a moment of happiness and hope for the best, like any other single woman would after the most fantastic first date in history.

Twenty-eight

Lucas

To meet Vivian every morning for breakfast, I have to push my running sessions to the evenings and add an extra mile to burn off all those donuts.

But even with all the saturated fats, I've never felt better.

By Friday, both Max and I have completely settled into this new routine. He initially resented me the lack of our morning jog, but once he understood we were simply shifting it to the evenings and not canceling altogether, he got on board.

Speaking of dogs, as I step into the elevator over lunch break on Friday, the redhead I spotted so long ago entering the offices of Inceptor Magazine is back. She follows me into the elevator, pulling along the cutest Labrador-ish puppy on a sparkly red leash.

The lady looks a lot less posh than she did just a few weeks ago. Correction: she's still fashionable, only in a sportier way rather than glamorous.

But the puppy is the real showstopper. I can't help myself; I squat down and pat the dog, asking, "Who is this beauty?"

"Her name's Chevron," the redhead gushes. "I found her at a gas station the other day, and now I've adopted her. Co-adopted, rather, with my boss. Isn't that crazy?"

And before I can answer yes or no, she continues. "Richard is supposedly a commitment-phobe, but would a true commitment-phobe offer to share custody of a dog? I mean, it's a multiyear undertaking, isn't it?"

Am I expected to answer? I straighten up and get back to eye level with her. Well, not really, since she's about a foot shorter than me.

"And now we're flying to LA, tonight. It's completely professional, of course." She air-quotes professional. "But don't you think it's weird he's asked me to go to a Hollywood gala instead of Ada, when she's the one in charge of entertainment? It would've made more sense, wouldn't it?"

She framed it like a question, but I'm certain she's not expecting an answer. Sure enough, she keeps rambling.

"Wow, this week has been crazy. First the dog, then going to jail, and now this impromptu work trip to the west coast."

She air-quotes work, like the nature of her west coast trip should be the focal point of her story, when all I want to know is how the heck she ended up in jail. But I'm scared to ask, should my query prompt another stream of nonsense.

Then the redhead stares me directly in the eye. "Do you think LA is more romantic than New York?"

And since this is a direct question, I feel compelled to give my two cents. "Is your boss the tall man with the British accent?"

Her eyes go wide—with surprise, or with fear? "You know Richard? You didn't tell me you knew him!"

"I don't, I've just seen him in passing," I say. Heck, if I were a woman, I'd probably be lusting after him, too. "Anyway," I add, "it's never a good idea to have a crush in the office, especially not on the big boss."

Her cheeks catch fire and turn a shade of red that matches her hair. "I absolutely *do not have* a crush on my boss."

The freight elevator finally stops on the ground floor, and

the doors magically open on the object of our conversation, Mr. Tall and British. The woman's cheeks grow redder, if that's even possible.

"Blair," the man greets her with a sheepish smile. "Glad I could catch you before you left."

I excuse myself and walk past them, thinking, *well, at least the crush is reciprocated.*

***

On Saturday afternoon, I whistle happily as I moonwalk into my bedroom to get changed for my date with Vivian. *Old Time Rock & Roll* by Bob Seger is playing on my phone, and I do a silly dance a la Tom Cruise in *Risky Business* as I yank clothes off the hangers in my closet. Today has been a stellar day. I ran 10k this morning, ate a healthy salad for lunch, and took a power nap. But I'm hoping tonight will be even better.

For our second date, I've vowed to get to the restaurant on time—ahead, even—and I want to have enough of a buffer to pick up flowers on the way.

Too much?

Nah, Vivian deserves roses by the dozens.

I'm about to pull off my sweatshirt when my phone rings. I'm half-tempted to let the call go unanswered but check the caller ID just in case.

My heart stops. It's the one person in the world I can't hang up on.

Twenty-nine

Vivian

Fifteen past eight, and still no sign of Lucas.

For someone who takes pride in being such a good-mannered gentleman, he sure has a knack for showing up late to dates.

When, another ten minutes later, a server comes asking for the third time if I'm doing okay and if I would like to order something to drink, I ask for a glass of white and check my phone—dead, out of battery.

How long has it been this way? Has Lucas tried to call me?

Impatient, I get up and go to the bathroom, where I discretely plug in the charger to a socket near the sinks and wait for the phone to power up.

The moment the screen comes to life, a million notifications pop up—all from Lucas.

I read the first text.

> Sorry, something came up, a
> work emergency. I'm going
> to be a little late

At once, my bullshit radar goes off. A work emergency? On a Saturday night? Lucas is a couples' therapist—I don't see any circumstance that would require him to meet with clients on a weekend. What did he have to do? Stop a plates-throwing fight between spouses in the name of saving fine china?

I don't think so. Makes no sense.

The second text is even worse.

> This will take longer than
> expected, I'm not sure if I'll
> be able to make it at all

The time stamp of this last message reads 7:30.

Did Lucas cancel our date by text thirty minutes before we were supposed to meet?

So much for good manners. I wouldn't show so little respect, not even for Roger's mother.

After a steadying breath, I read the rest.

> I'm so sorry, I was really
> looking forward to spending
> tonight with you

> I promise I'll make it up to
> you

Ah, he's sorry. Because that makes everything okay. *Want to prove you care? Show. Up.*

I'm so mad, I'm tempted to delete his last messages without even reading them. But I'm not that firm, so I read on.

> Vivian? I tried to call you but
> your phone is off

> I hope you're not at the restaurant already
>
> I'm doing my best to get to you, but traffic is horrible tonight
>
> Please forgive me, I don't know how to apologize

Don't bother, I reply in my head.

This is what I deserve for opening up to a man again. Our first real date, and he stands me up with some half-assed excuse that makes no sense.

Lucas never struck me as the lying type, but then again, neither had Tegan's father. Maybe there's something wrong with me. I must be genetically programmed to only be attracted to bastards.

And, okay, Lucas blowing me off for a date is not the same as my daughter's father telling her to her face that he wants nothing to do with her. But Lucas knows how hard it is for me to trust, to be vulnerable, to put my happiness into somebody else's hands. And on the first occasion he has to prove he cares about me, he's a no show.

Disappointed in a way that aches inside, I unplug the phone and go back to my table. The wine has arrived; I take a long sip, and then ask for the bill, doing my best to ignore the pitying look the server spares me.

I pay in cash to be quicker, grab my coat, and march straight out of the restaurant, hoping I won't have to wait too long for a free cab.

I'm pacing up and down the curb, searching the street for a free taxi, when a car screeches to a halt on the other side of the road—Lucas' SUV.

He gets out in a rush, all flustered—the opposite of how I feel. A cold calm has settled over me. I trusted him, and I was wrong. End of story.

The walls I'd struggled to let down are back up, strengthened with new fortifications I won't let any man through ever again.

"Vivian." He stops in front of me, panting. "I'm so sorry."

He's wearing a fleece sweatshirt and sweatpants. Riiight, he had a work emergency. Like he would be caught dead in front of his clients wearing anything less than a three-piece suit.

"No problem," I say, falsely cheerful. "You had a work emergency, right?"

Lucas seems relieved. "Yes, totally out of the blue, and I'm so sorry I couldn't let you know before. You must hate me right now—"

"What kind of emergency?"

His eyes get wary. "I can't discuss clients."

"How convenient. See, I could understand if you worked in a psychiatric ward with people in serious trouble who could have *emergencies*. But you're a couples' therapist, so I'm curious as to what happened for you to have to drop everything and stand me up on a Saturday night."

"I can't tell you."

"Ah, going 'no comment' all the way. Like a real pro."

"A pro what?"

"Liar."

"I'm not lying."

"So you were out saving a marriage tonight?"

Lucas stares at me. "No."

"What were you doing, then?"

"I can't tell you," he repeats.

Behind him, I spot a cab with the light on coming our way. I stomp off the curb and raise my arm to stop it.

Before getting in, I turn to Lucas, who looks lost and desperate. "Then we have nothing more to say to each other. I don't want a man who can't be honest with me."

"Vivian, wait!" he calls after me, as I slam the door. "Please!"

I turn my head away from him as the taxi pulls into the street.

***

While making my exit, I might've acted like a strong, resolute woman. But inside the cab, I break down. Tears flood my eyes and I can't stop the sobs.

I'm so pathetic. I'd sworn I'd never stoop this low for a man ever again, and yet, here I am.

At home, I kick my shoes off in the hall and then check on Tegan, opening her door a crack. The faint sound of her snoring greets me.

I open the door a tad more and slip inside to steal the cat from the foot of Tegan's bed. Tonight, I need some company.

In my room, I drop Priscilla on the bed and move into the bathroom to remove my makeup with jerky, angry moves. So much for the effort. I shouldn't have bothered.

What's even sadder is when I shimmy out of the sexy underwear I picked out especially for him. What a waste of lace. I switch to sensible, cotton panties, pull on an oversized T-shirt, and scoot under the covers.

Priscilla raises her head threateningly, a warning not to disturb her slumber a second time. I disregard her silent protest and hug her closer to my chest, scratching her behind the ears.

The purring starts, and slowly lulls me to sleep.

***

For a week, I do my best to ignore Lucas. I ignore his calls, his texts, and the three bouquets of roses he sends me. I get to the office before him, and don't leave until his SUV has disappeared from the street.

And the one time he comes knocking on my door, I stubbornly pretend not to be there. Lucas knows I'm inside— he yells it through the door—but I purse my lips and refuse to let him in. He's no longer welcome in my office, my life, and, most importantly, my heart.

The avoidance strategy works pretty well, until I meet with Leslie for drinks on Friday night and she forces me to stare at the facts. We're on a rooftop in Manhattan with a wonderful view of the city, drinking overpriced strawberry martinis.

"Are you sure you didn't overreact?" my friend asks. "Luke tried to cancel the date, didn't he? He didn't stand you up on purpose."

"With a text, thirty minutes before we were supposed to meet. Who does that?"

"But he said it was a work emergency."

"What kind of work emergency? He was wearing sweat pants, and when I asked him if he was out saving a marriage, he admitted he wasn't. That's literally his job. All he *does* is save marriages."

"It could've been something else he can't tell you about."

"Yeah, like what?"

Leslie takes a sip of her martini, pondering the question. "I have no idea."

"Neither do I. I've tried for a week to come up with a plausible explanation that isn't shady, but I couldn't think of anything."

"Okay," Leslie agrees. "But Lucas is the least shady person I know. And you haven't felt this way about anyone in... Well, have you ever?"

Truthfully, no. Not even with Tegan's father; my relationship with him was never on an even plane. I was always kept in my place, and he reminded me constantly who the student and the professor were. It was subordinate. Unhealthy. Wrong.

But Lucas... Oh, he charmed me subtly, in a way I wasn't ready to handle. He bamboozled me. Gained my trust little by little, only to squander everything by being caught in a lie.

And the worst part is that Tegan already identifies him as a father figure. He didn't crush just me. He crushed the both of us, and I can never forgive him for that.

"Fine. I liked him, a lot. So what? How's that supposed to make it better? I just feel all the more duped."

"I'm telling you, Lucas is not the duping kind of guy," Leslie says firmly. "At least hear him out."

***

I carry Leslie's suggestion around with me all night as I toss in bed, not sleeping, and then all of Saturday as well. No matter how much I try to shake it off, she's planted a seed of doubt in my head.

Yes, I can't explain why Lucas lied, but if I analyze the time I've known him, there wasn't a single occasion in which he hasn't been completely honest with me. Well-behaved? Maybe not always. Especially not the first day we met when he yelled at me, but I'm blaming that on sugar deprivation. Don't touch the man's donuts, I've learned that much.

Is one lie worth closing the door on him forever?

The more I sit on it, the more uncertainty gnaws at me. Leslie has a point—I did rush in dismissing him. I should have given him a chance to explain. Well, I still can. And, like all important things, it should be done face to face.

Decision made, I'm in such a hurry to go that I don't even change into more decent clothes. Sweats were good enough for Lucas' so-called client emergency, and they'll do for an impromptu home visit.

Tegan has gone to the movies with friends again so, when I exit the house, I need nothing more than my bag and keys.

I have to ask Leslie for the address of Lucas' condo, as I never got as far as going to his place. And this time, I don't plan to do so in sexy lingerie. It gives me satisfaction that I'm wearing the oldest, crappiest underwear set I own. No, not even a set, as the bra and panties are mismatched.

The trip to lower Manhattan doesn't take too long on the subway, and his house is thankfully just a short walk from the station. I'm searching the front door of the building for a bell or something when the glass doors open and Lucas comes out.

"Vivian." His eyes widen at finding me on his doorstep.

He's dressed casually in jeans and a dark green sweater. And, damn him, if he doesn't look yummier than a triple-glazed donut, if those even exist.

"What are you doing here?" he asks.

"I wanted to talk."

Lucas tries to subtly check the time on his watch.

"Somewhere you have to be?" I ask.

He turns defensive. "As a matter of fact, yes."

"Another emergency you can't tell me about?"

"It isn't an emergency, but I still can't tell you where I'm going. But, Vivian"—he gently grabs my wrist—"I want to talk to you. There's nothing I want more."

I yank my arm free. "Don't bother. Coming here was a mistake."

"Vivian, please! I promise you I'm not doing anything wrong, I'm just protecting someone else's privacy."

"Who? A client?"

His lips go taut. "I really can't tell you any more than I already have. You have to trust me on this."

And there it is, hanging between us like a sword, the unspoken question I'm facing.

Can I trust him? Can I put blind faith into someone? A man?

If it were just me… maybe I could take the leap. But I can't think just about myself. I haven't for most of my adult life. Tegan's wellbeing will always come before anything else, and I can't bring another man into our lives who has secrets. However innocent he claims they are, I need total transparency in a relationship.

I shake my head. "Sorry, I can't."

Lucas' eyes turn sad. "Then you're right, we have nothing else to say to each other. Sorry, I have to go now."

Without another word, he crosses the street and walks away from me. And, I guess, out of my life for good. If that's what I was after, then why does it still hurt so much?

Thirty

Vivian

Three weeks later, I'm still nursing my heartbreak. The cure, I've decided, is excessive work during the day, and an endless stream of covert, late nights spent watching romantic movies and eating ice cream—the heavy stuff. To protect my daughter, I always wait until Tegan has gone to bed and can't see me before I start my sad nightly routine. But even if I've tried to maintain a strong façade in front of her, I'm not convinced she's bought my act. Lately, she never goes out except for movies with friends on Saturday nights, and why else would a teenager spend so much time at home if not to keep her heartbroken mother company?

Tonight, however, I must make more noise than usual, because halfway through my regular sob-fest, Tegan pokes her head into the living room.

She takes me in, along with the ice cream bucket I'm holding—I opted for the saving size package—and with a sigh she sits at the other end of the couch, chin bowed low.

"Mom, are you sad about Luke?" she asks without looking up.

"No, honey, I'm fine. It's just the movie."

Tegan stares at the screen, where *Forgetting Sarah Marshall* is playing. Hardly a tear-jerker. If my excuse wasn't paper thin enough already, I shift my legs on the couch and a Polaroid picture of Lucas falls on the carpet. I found the photo in Tegan's room and I couldn't resist. She must've taken it outside our office, I don't know when, and

Lucas just looks so handsome in it.

My daughter picks up the photo from the floor. "Why aren't you seeing him anymore?"

"It's complicated, honey, but the bottom line is I couldn't trust him."

"For what it's worth, Mom, I really like him. He'd make a great stepdad."

This affirmation pulls on all the wrong strings and makes my heart break into even smaller pieces.

"Baby, I know he seems..." I don't know what I want to say... Amazing? Reliable? Perfect? "Look, when I had you, I promised myself I'd never let someone I couldn't depend on one hundred percent into our lives. I won't make an exception for Lucas."

"Why don't you trust him? Is it because he didn't show up for your second date?"

The hair at the back of my neck prickles. I never share details of my private life with my daughter, exactly because I don't want my burdens to become hers. Especially not since Lucas is still her therapist and is helping her cope with her father's rejection better than I could've ever hoped. So how does she know I was stood up? I didn't tell her. Did he? Did he use their sessions to offload himself on her, instead of facilitating her recovery? Did Lucas put her up to this?

With a heart suddenly made of steel, I ask, "How do you know Lucas stood me up? Did the two of you discuss it?"

"No."

"Then how?"

"Mom." Tegan looks up, her eyes streaked with tears and big with fear. Why is she afraid? "I have to tell you something," she continues in a wobbly voice, "but can you please promise not to send me off to boarding school?"

I stiffen on my side of the couch. "You know I can't make that promise," I say, trying to keep my tone even and calm. "If you have something to confess, be ready to accept the consequences."

"Okay." She swallows and looks back at the carpet. "Remember the night of your second date with Luke, when I told you I was going to the movies with Jesse and to maybe grab a bite to eat later?"

"Yes?"

"It was a lie. We went to a house party in the Upper East Side. Our friend Josh's parents were away for the weekend and he and his older brother were hosting, so Jesse's sister was invited as well."

I grip the couch cushions to prevent myself from screaming. I want to hear the full story first, and she'll never tell me if I start shouting. So I keep quiet as Tegan spills out the rest.

"We went on the subway together, and we agreed we'd split a cab home. When we got to Josh's house... there was... alcohol at the party..."

I grip harder.

"I had a beer or two, and I was totally fine."

I swear, the casualty with which Tegan says she drinks beer is killing me, but still, I remain silent.

"But then someone brought in Jell-O shots, and I know I shouldn't have drunk those, but everyone else was, and I didn't want to look lame, so I did a few, and I was fine at first, but after half an hour I started to get really sick so I asked Jesse and Josie to take me home."

My heart is beating so fast it might explode.

"But Josie didn't want to go because there was a boy she liked at the party, and Jesse does whatever her older sister tells her, you know how she is. I didn't have enough money to pay for a cab on my own, and you don't want me to ride the subway at night alone, and I wasn't feeling well enough anyway."

"Why didn't you call me?" I manage to ask, half-choked with anxiety.

Tegan stares at me now, tears streaming down her cheeks. "Mom, you would've gotten so mad. You lost it last time over a single sip of vodka; what would you have done if I called drunk from a house party you had no idea I was going to?"

Okay, I would've probably flown off the handle. But that's beside the point.

"So, what did you do?"

Torn with guilt, she says, "I called Luke."

My heart breaks and heals a million times in the space of a second. *Tegan* was the emergency he couldn't talk about?

"And, Mom, I made him swear not to tell you anything, or else I wouldn't give him the address."

The guilt of not trusting him punches me in the stomach, while my pulse accelerates further.

"And then what happened?" I ask, close to tears myself.

"Well, he dropped everything—namely you and your date—and came to get me. It wasn't that late yet, so Luke thought he'd make it to dinner in time. But then, while we were driving home, I felt sick and we had to stop. He got me a Gatorade at a 7-Eleven, and it took me a while to be okay again. We were still in the car when he called you, but your phone was off or something. Anyway, once I was well enough to go back in the car, he brought me home, put me to bed, and made sure I was sleeping before he came to you."

On one hand, I'm deeply touched by how he took care of my daughter. I feel like a complete idiot, and I want to run after Lucas to beg him to forgive me. On the other hand, I can't help being furious that he'd keep such a huge secret from me. This is my *daughter* we're talking about; when a teen pulls a stunt like that, it's not okay to just put them to bed, make sure they're all right, and leave them with no consequences.

"And that's it? He put you to bed, and promised not to tell me anything?"

Tegan wrings her fingers. "I think Luke wanted me to realize the right thing to do was to tell you myself."

A memory of the hurt look in his eyes when I said I couldn't trust him haunts me. The toll to keep silent must've been high, at least if his feelings were as strong as mine. Are they, still? I put a pin in that thought to analyze it later. Right now, I need to deal with my daughter.

"And in the meantime, you just walked free?"

"No, Mom. I'm grounded."

I stare at her. "I didn't ground you."

"Luke did." She begins listing her punishments. "No phone, no laptop except for homework, and no going out save for volleyball games."

I wondered why she was still using that relic of a phone I gave her, when her grounding was supposed to have ended weeks ago.

"That's not true," I say. "You've been going to the movies each Saturday for a month."

"No, Mom, Luke has been taking me to AA meetings for

endangered teens," Tegan says this with a slight roll of her eyes, as if she still thinks everyone's overreacting. But in my head, another penny drops.

"He's been spending *all* his Saturday nights with you?"

"Yes, Mom, and he has season tickets to the Knicks, so he can't be too happy about it."

"Wait, so the Saturday after the party, Lucas was with you?"

"I told you, it's part of our deal."

My mind is racing. "So when I went to his house, he must've been on his way to meet you?"

"You went to see him?"

"Yes, and I made an even bigger ass of myself." I get up, suddenly not able to sit for a second longer. "You're grounded," I tell Tegan. "Well, more grounded than you already are."

She nods, resigned. "I know, Mom."

"And we're going to discuss everything that's happened—"

"I'd figured…"

"—when I come back. But I need to go now."

She follows me into the hall as I throw on a pair of Uggs over my leggings and grab my keys.

I put on my coat, open the front door, and point a finger at my daughter. "Do not leave the house for *any* reason." I pause, reconsidering. "Unless there's a fire or something."

"Go, Mom, and don't worry about me. I'm going to bed, and I know I won't be allowed to go out again until I'm eighteen."

Tegan says it half as a joke, but I tend to agree with her. It will take a long time before I'll trust her again.

I walk down the street with a plan in mind. I have to trudge a few blocks before I find a place that's still open this late, but I finally succeed.

Armed with the best please-forgive-me bribe a woman can have, I hail a free cab and give the driver Lucas' address.

Thirty-one

Lucas

When the buzzer of my apartment goes off, I'm already in bed, busy not sleeping and staring at the ceiling, wallowing in my usual cloud of self-despair.

The alarm clock on the bedside table informs me it's almost midnight. Who would ring me this late at night? A neighbor who forgot his keys?

I get up, walk into the living room, and press the intercom button. "Yes?"

"I have a delivery," a weird voice says from the other side. I can't tell if it's male or female.

"You have the wrong apartment. I didn't order anything."

"Are you Lucas Keller?"

"Yes?"

"Then there's a delivery for you."

"What is it?"

"I'm just a messenger, sir."

"Okay, come up, I'm in apartment 4B."

As I wait for the delivery person to arrive, I don't open the front door, but wait behind it, spying from the peephole. A delivery at midnight for something I didn't order? Sounds highly suspicious. It could be a robbery attempt, or a prank, or...

My eyes bulge.

Or it could be Vivian, looking entirely scruffy-dressed and messy-haired but none the less beautiful as she walks down the hall carrying a small box in her hands.

I throw the door open. "Did you just pretend to be a delivery guy?"

She jumps back, frightened at my sudden appearance, but recovers quickly. "I didn't pretend." Vivian shows me the box. "I have a delivery for you."

"So you didn't change your voice."

"The intercom must have a strong distortion."

I cross my arms and lean against the doorframe, as Max peeks curiously from between my legs.

"And what's in the bag, Miss I'm Just a Messenger, sir?"

"Donuts," she says.

"Who would send me a box of donuts so late at night?"

She gets closer, but not too close. "Someone who's really sorry she couldn't trust you when she should have and wants to apologize?"

With an outstretched leg, I stop Max from running into the hall to cover Vivian in doggy kisses—which, to be honest, is what I'd like to do right now. Well, maybe not the doggy part.

I try to keep cool as I say, "Tegan finally confessed?"

"Yes, and Lucas, I'm sorry for the way I reacted, but it really did make no sense you'd have to work on a Saturday night. I'm a lawyer, remember? I need facts and logic. And neither was adding up, so I panicked. The last time I gave myself completely to someone—"

"I'm nothing like that man," I cut her off.

"I know you aren't. You've been more of a father to Tegan in the past two months than he has all her life. But being with him left me burned... And with trust issues, I'm aware."

I do my best to keep to my side of the hall and fight the

instinct of wrapping my arms around her and kissing her.

"What if something else like this happens?" I ask. "I'm bound by doctor-patient confidentiality, Vivian, and occasionally there *will* be emergencies. Will you bail on me again the next time you get suspicious?"

"Well, I hope you'll never have to go pick up my drunk daughter at a secret party ever again." I'm about to protest, when she adds, "But even if something different happened that you couldn't tell me about, I swear I won't run. I can't promise I won't get mad, but I won't cop out." Vivian takes a deep breath. "I mistook you not coming to our date as a sign you didn't care enough. But what I hadn't realized is that you've been showing up for me—and Tegan—for as long as we've known you." She pauses again. "Except maybe for that first day at the office."

I raise an eyebrow in a "Do you really want to go there?" way.

She falters. "What I'm trying to say is that, except being a lunatic about donuts, you've pushed and shoved your way into my heart, and now I couldn't get you out even if I wanted to."

"But you want me out?"

"No, I don't." Vivian shakes her head vigorously. "I want you in, so in... That is, I mean, if you still want me?"

The vulnerability in her voice makes me crack. Who am I kidding? She could've come here and told me, "You take me back right now, you dumb fool," and I would have agreed without a second thought.

She's suffered enough. *I've* suffered enough.

I relax my shoulders and straighten away from the doorframe, taking a step toward her. "Can I say you had me at donuts?"

"Really? Because you were grilling me pretty heavily a second ago."

"I had to play a little hard to get, didn't I? Plus, when am I ever going to hear you say again that you're wrong?"

"I never said I was wrong. I said I was sorry, and that I have trust issues."

"Still, you were groveling."

"I was apologizing, in a totally dignified way."

"Apology accepted," I say, taking the box of donuts from her hands and dropping it on the hall's cabinet. I pull her inside the condo and shut the door behind us. "And now I want to kiss you, and I'm asking in a totally undignified way. Do you have any objections, counselor?"

Vivian's smile is bright as she throws her arms around my neck. "Not a one."

Epilog

Max

My human has been weird lately. First, we had that week when Luke switched our routine and we ran in the evening instead of early mornings. I didn't mind; the jogs lasted longer, and we had fun. Then, we had a month of total despair, when running was out of the question and I barely managed to get him off the couch for a walk in the park. And now we have this new phase...

The daily runs are back—which is good, but I'm seriously worried about Luke. He's not himself anymore. He's always distracted, can't stop smiling like an idiot for more than two minutes, and he's constantly humming or whistling under his breath—which is a little annoying.

And then there's the woman. The beautiful one who stinks of cat.

She's around the house an awful lot, and even when she isn't, I can still smell her and her cat on Luke.

We've had one of those human females in our lives before, and let me tell you, it didn't end well. Brenda stuck around for two years and then left out of the blue, leaving my buddy in tatters. And now that he's finally recovered, here comes another. I'm worried, I'm not gonna lie. From the way Luke is behaving, if this one were ever to leave, I can't even imagine how many days we'd go without runs in the park.

There's also a younger human in the picture who I don't mind as much. She cuddles me the most, gives me a lot of food from her plate when she comes over for dinner, and she takes lots of pictures of me. Tegan brings me out on the longest walks while she takes pictures of the most random things. She's the best.

And maybe I'm not being fair to her mother; it's just that I'm wary when it comes to my human pal and these *women*.

But, really, the worst part is Luke constantly whistling. I wish he would stop.

And, as if by magic, he does.

I stare up at Luke as he stops abruptly in our small entrance hall. We're back from a stroll in the park after lunch—it's one of those days the humans named "weekend," which means Luke didn't disappear to a place called "work" all day—and Luke is checking the post, reading a sheet of paper out of one of those white envelopes.

The more he reads, the more he frowns. And when he finishes, Luke walks into the living room, phone in hand.

Hey!

He forgot to untie my leash.

I bark.

I don't want to drag this thing around the house, it constantly gets tangled underneath my paws and it can become a real nuisance.

Luke ignores me. He sits on the couch and, while re-reading the letter, makes a call.

"Hey, Sweetheart..."

Of course, it's her.

"Yeah, would you mind coming over a little earlier?"

She says something, and Luke chuckles.

"I'd like that very much but, no, I need legal advice."

More indistinct murmuring on the other side.

"My building has been sold," Luke says. "And they're

asking all the tenants to move out, so I wanted to check my legal options."

They talk a while longer, until Luke finally hangs up.

I bark again.

Lucas pats me distractedly on the head while he rereads that stupid letter for the third time. "Not now, buddy, I'm busy."

And I'm stuck with a potential choking hazard around my neck!

I pick up the red leash with my mouth and stand up on my hind legs, whining pitifully.

Luke looks up and finally notices my discomfort.

"Sorry, pal," he says, unhooking the leash. "I forgot."

Relieved of the dreadful contraption, I sink down on all fours, sighing. What a dog has to do to get noticed these days.

I sure preferred the bachelor life.

***

A few hours later, the woman arrives. Her name's Sweetheart, or at least that's what Lucas calls her. She's wearing a nice dress and perfume, meaning they plan to get their food outside. I don't care much for the flowery scent, but if nothing else it covers some of the cat stink.

Tonight, though, something is different. Instead of going out right away as they usually do, they sit at the small kitchen table in their fancy clothes, studying the same letter Luke was obsessing over earlier.

"They can't force me out, can they?" Luke is saying. "Even if the building changed owners, I still have a signed lease. The new landlord can't cancel the contract, right?"

"No one's forcing you to leave; they're asking you *nicely.*

Two months rent-free to find a new place isn't a bad offer."

"But I don't want to move!"

"When does your lease expire?"

"July next year."

The woman thinks for a second, as if making calculations. "So we're talking about an eight-month difference at best, since they won't renew your lease come July. Is that worth putting up a fight?"

"Fight? What fight? If I refuse their offer, I don't have to move for almost a year, and that's that. No fight."

"Okay, but assume it's just you and a few other tenants staying. The landlord could make your life unpleasant."

"Legally or illegally?"

"I'm not saying they'll redo your floors with carpet infested by bed bugs, like in *Suits,* but there are plenty of other ways to make you uncomfortable."

"Like what?"

"The new management could shut down the common amenities, saying it's not feasible to keep them open for only a few people. Think of this place with no gym, no laundry room, no doorman. Would you still like to live here?"

Grim, Luke shakes his head.

"Or, even worse," she continues. "They could start the renovation with you still inside the building. Trust me, a week with construction workers as your neighbors and you'll be fleeing the place faster than you can blink. The noise of a jackhammer is legal torture, and you can't stop them."

Luke brandishes the letter. "So, is this my best option?"

"I'm sorry, but, yes."

"Well, I'd better call Leslie right away." Luke sags against the back of the chair. "First my office, and now my house, both in the same year. I'm going to have nightmares about carton boxes and moving trucks."

"May I suggest *I* park the rental truck this time?" A teasing tone laces her voice. "And I hope it wasn't all bad for you, changing offices."

"Well," Luke says, that ridiculous dumb-struck, fool-in-love expression on his face. "I didn't find a corner office, but I found you. I won't get that lucky twice."

Sweetheart smiles. "You'd better not."

"Man, I hate hunting for apartments. I hope at least residential is less complicated than commercial."

"What if you didn't have to look for a new place?"

"You just told me I have no choice."

"No, you have to move, but what if you already had a place to stay?" Sweetheart bites on a fingernail, looking uncertain. "I have such a huge house; I always thought it was too big for Tegan and me."

Luke's eyes shine. "Are you asking me to move in with you?"

Into the stinky cat house? Are they crazy?

"Yes," she says. "We could be a real family, and it'd be the best Christmas present ever for Tegan. And for me."

I turn to Luke; he's staring at her with a weird expression. Good to see we're on the same page. This relationship is advancing way too fast. And moving in together after only a few months? No thank you. We'll stay right here, far away from any and all stinky cats.

"I know we'd have less privacy with Tegan always around," Sweetheart continues, and I assume she's referring to the times they close themselves in the bedroom and make weird noises. "But you've already moved your practice to

Brooklyn, and you'd be closer to work, and—"

Luke silences her, pressing a finger to her mouth. He's probably trying to find a way to turn her down gently.

"You don't have to sell it to me," he says. "I would love nothing more than to live with you and Tegan."

What?

Has he completely lost his mind? Luke can't seriously expect me to share a house with a cat. He left me there for an entire day once, and the stench almost killed me—dogs have a very sensitive sense of smell.

They stand up, embrace, and kiss.

Once they break apart, Sweetheart glances at her watch, saying, "We'd better go now, or we'll be late for our reservation."

I'm still reeling from the awful turn my life has taken— cohabitation with a cat, a canine nightmare—when I realize they've forgotten about me.

I run into the hall, barking.

"What's up, buddy?" Luke asks. "Don't worry, we'll be back in a few hours."

Not the problem, dude.

I keep barking.

"Did you feed him?" Sweetheart asks. "Max looks hungry."

At least one of the humans still has some functioning cells in her brain.

"Oh, gosh, you're right. I didn't," Luke says, bending down to scratch me. "Sorry, I don't know where my head is these days."

But I do, and it has lots to do with big brown eyes and a pretty human face.

235

Priscilla

The holidays are usually my favorite time of the year. The weather outside gets cold, but inside my heated, cozy home I don't have to worry about the snow. And, from time to time, the humans I live with even light the fireplace, which gives me the perfect space to curl up next to. Tegan and Vivian also put up a tree filled with shiny colored decorations I can play with. There are extra warm blankets to knead. More cuddles for no reason. And on the most special day they call Christmas, plenty of discarded ribbons and paper balls to chase around the house.

Not this year.

My life is ruined.

Ever since that dog moved in.

This used to be a sanctuary, a three-gal show made of quiet days spent by myself as the queen of the house and cozy nights on the couch watching romantic movies. Everything was ordered, feminine, perfect…

And now everything smells of dog. Oh, the stench alone is enough for me to have considered moving homes on multiple occasions. I even went as far as running away a few times, but then I thought of my Tegan, and I couldn't leave for good. Plus, I got hungry. And at least, when I came back, they all appreciated me more.

Anyway, my problem isn't only with the doggy smell; that awful pooch has invaded every single one of my spaces. In the kitchen, his food bowls are next to mine—and he pretends not to, but I know he drinks from my water bowl when he thinks I can't see him. Ew, his slosh is gross. In Tegan's room, he wants to sleep on the bed with us at night, and the worst part is that she lets him. And in the living room, Max always tries to sit in my favorite armchair.

Over my dead body. I clawed him good the first time he tried, and whenever he gets close to it, I jump in before he can—he's pretty slow for someone who trains with daily runs—and hiss him away.

Besides the dog, there's the human male, Lucas. He is Vivian's mate, and the one responsible for bringing that dreadful mutt into our lives. I want to be mad at him. I try. Every time he puts his hands on me, I swear to myself I won't purr, but then he starts his magic and, damn me, I purr my heart out for him every single time. His fingers are out of this world; he scratches my ears like no one else. Heck, I have it on good authority humans are not supposed to purr, but he can make even Vivian purr with those devilish hands of his. I've witnessed it with my own eyes—I can see in the dark.

Lucas is not hard to look at, either. I'm not an expert in humans' aesthetic standards, but even I can tell he's a catch. And, in his favor, he has mounted a special perch for me up on the wall with a walkway underneath where I can hide whenever the dog is bothering me too much. I preferred to have the whole house, but it's a start. Plus, the cat bed up there is plush and heated, which was a nice touch. This Lucas guy surely knows how to treat his ladies. I've never seen Vivian so smiley, and even Tegan loves him; she seems much more carefree since he's moved in.

Ah, yes, it pains me to admit it, but he's making my humans happier, so the dog is a necessary evil I'll have to learn to live with—except if he tries to get on my armchair. Then I'll claw his stupid nose off.

In my Christmas letter for Santa this year, I'll ask that

they bathe him more often. Dogs are so dirty.

I stroll into the kitchen now while Lucas and Vivian are having breakfast. On the weekends, since the two males have moved in, there's bacon sometimes, which I'll admit is one of the few nice novelties. As I brush against Lucas' legs, he scratches me behind the ears and then hand-feeds me a scrap of bacon—double purr. I hop on a chair to annoy Max; he isn't allowed to. Having the high ground, I make sure the dog is watching me and then give Lucas a head-bump on the arm—Max hates it when I cuddle his human.

The dog promptly growls from under the table. Aha, take that, you dirty, smelly canine.

"Max, be a good boy," Lucas says, and feeds him some bacon.

I swear, that dog is too dumb to keep an attention span of more than a few seconds. He scarfs down his bacon and yaps away happily. Really, I shouldn't even engage with such an inferior creature.

Lucas coughs. "Sweetheart," he says, handing Vivian the tablet he was holding in his hands. "There's an article you might want to read."

Vivian takes the tablet and stares at the screen. "*The Boston Globe?*" Then, as her eyes travel down the page, she gasps. "Oh my gosh, how did you—?"

"I've been keeping an eye out since you sent those letters. Took them long enough, uh?"

Vivian stands up abruptly, all but sending her chair crashing down. "I have to tell Tegan," she says, and drops the tablet on the table.

"She's sleeping. Let her rest. You can tell her when she wakes up."

"I'm sure she won't mind me waking her up for this."

Vivian is about to exit the kitchen, but she changes her mind halfway. She turns back, rounds the table, and covers Lucas' face with kisses. "I love you." Then she's gone.

I stare at Lucas, who for once looks as dumb as his dog. Unbelievable. I shift my gaze to the tablet still lying on the table to investigate what the fuss is about.

A picture of a handsome man with blue-gray eyes and dark hair whitening at the temples occupies half the page, while the rest is covered in those black symbols humans seem to make sense of, but that I never found very useful.

Two minutes later, Tegan drags her feet into the kitchen still wearing her pajamas and, rubbing sleep from her eyes with her fists, she plonks on a chair. I immediately chair hop and jump onto her legs, bumping my head under her chin. She scratches me in return.

"So, Mom, what is this news that couldn't wait a few hours? Are you pregnant or something?"

Vivian blushes red from head to toe. "No, honey."

"Okay, can I have a cup of coffee first?"

Lucas stands up and fills a mug for her. Then, from the still-hot skillet, he piles a plate with bacon and eggs and places it in front of Tegan, saying, "For the princess of the house." He ruffles her hair affectionately.

Tegan swats him away, fake annoyed. Then she stares at her mom as she takes a sip of coffee. "So?"

Vivian picks up the tablet again and starts reading aloud. "Harvard Dean of Humanities being let go after several sexual harassment allegations came to light. Criminal charges might be brought forward as a thorough investigation from the Boston Police Department is underway."

Tegan squeezes me close to her chest. "Was it us, Mom? Keep reading."

"'Allegations about sexual misconduct by Professor Robert J. Preston were first brought before the Harvard Faculty Board by an undisclosed source,' our informant within the Arts & Humanities Department at Harvard University tells us. After the accusations were received, Dean Preston was immediately put on a leave of absence while the renowned college performed a thorough investigation. News travels fast in the academic circles, and soon more women came forward with stories of power abuse, threats, and unwanted advances—"

Tegan interrupts at this point. "I knew it couldn't be just us, Mom. He was so arrogant with me, so sure of himself, like someone who's used to getting away with everything. But, sorry, keep reading."

Vivian, who seems very emotional right now, grabs her daughter's hand across the table and continues, "'Not being alone gave me the strength to come forward,' says Beatrix Montgomery, one of the accusing women, who claims to have been fired from her administrative job after ending her relationship with Preston. 'I always thought no one would believe me, but seeing other women tell the truth empowered me to speak up about what happened to me.' Beatrix then wanted to express her gratitude for the brave woman who spurred the investigation." Vivian drops the tablet and stands up. "That's you, Tegan."

Tegan gets up as well to hug her mother, and I don't even mind that I'm carelessly dropped to the floor in the move— we cats always land on our feet.

Vivian is crying now. "You're such a brave young woman. I'm so proud of you."

Lucas joins them in the hug. "We're both proud of you."

I stare at the three of them, clasped in the sweetest three-way hug, and, gosh, if they don't make for a beautiful family.

Max

Priscilla is warming up to me. Okay, there was that one time when she caught me drinking from her water bowl and threw a tantrum and basically destroyed the kitchen. But other than that, she's fine with me. Mostly. I can tell Prissy is being more playful than spiteful when she tries to annoy me. Like when she curls into Luke, or when she sits at the dinner table just because she knows I can't, or whenever she disappears into that special cat-bed of hers up on the wall.

It's even been two whole months since she ran away last, a few days into the New Year. What an attention-seeking cat drama queen. Oh, the fuss she created with every disappearing act! She stayed out long enough to get the humans into a frenzy, only to show up on the porch a few hours later as if nothing had happened. I still have to figure out how she does it. How does she leave the house without the humans letting her out?

Maybe that's also why she escaped; she was jealous I get to go on daily runs and walks in the park, while she's stuck at home all day long. Take that time the whole family drove north for a day-trip in the woods: Priscilla was the only one left behind. I felt awful for her, as it was a super amazing day—even if Vivian complained a bit toward the end of the hike and made Luke swear that next weekend they were going for a spa break, whatever that is.

Anyway, Priscilla and I are fine now. Well, unless I try to sleep on her precious armchair. Then she gets all surly with me again.

Priscilla is curled up there now, looking all territorial, while the humans watch TV on the couch.

I stroll past the armchair, and her eyes narrow. I ignore her and hop on the free end of the couch, joining the humans. It's fun to keep Prissy on her toes like that; she never knows when I'll try to dethrone her. In our friendly domestic war, the element of surprise is essential.

I curl up on the cushions and concentrate on the TV. A sad-looking woman is riding on a train while nothing much is happening.

"Hey," Luke says out of the blue. "I never asked you why you chose Miss Pocahontas as your alias."

Vivian turns to him. "It's from *Notting Hill*."

Luke's stare remains blank.

"The movie," Vivian prompts him. "You haven't seen it?"

"No, sorry."

"We have to watch it, it's one of my favorites. Anyway, Julia Roberts is this American mega movie star and she falls in love with bookstore owner Hugh Grant in Notting Hill." Vivian flaps her hands in the air. "Complications. Complications. Complications."

Luke smiles. "I like your narrative style."

"In the final act, when Julia Roberts is back in London, Hugh Grant needs to find her. He knows which hotel she's staying at, but the concierge won't tell him which room unless he says the right name. Anna, the character, always uses an alias because she's so famous and all, and all he knows is it's from a cartoon. So in this funny scene, Hugh Grant keeps yelling silly names, but never gets the right character. So, the concierge takes pity on him and tells him."

"Let me guess: Miss Pocahontas?"

"Yep."

He pokes her nose. "You're cute."

At that point, the woman on the TV starts screaming, and they both return their attention to the screen.

"I don't like this movie," Vivian says. "Can we watch something happy?"

Luke looks down at her. "*Notting Hill?*"

Vivian beams and grabs the remote. "Let me see if it's available on demand."

Aww, they're so cute.

***

The next morning, I'm headed to the kitchen to join the humans for breakfast when, passing in the hall, I notice the living room armchair is empty.

Mmm.

Kitty, kitty, kitty, where are you?

I could ruffle Priscilla's fur a little.

But where is she? I trot into the living room and find her sprawled underneath the TV stand. Perfect. From the floor, she has a wonderful view of the armchair.

I parade in front of her, the image of a perfectly innocent dog. Then, as soon as I've made it look like I'm about to exit again, I do a one-eighty and hop on the armchair, releasing a bark of victory.

From her hiding place, Priscilla barely lifts her head, then drops it back on the floor, letting out a pitiful meow.

Something is wrong.

I jump off the armchair at once and go sniff closer to her. Again, she makes a feeble attempt to claw at me, but drops her paw halfway, clearly in pain.

I know what to do.

I rush into the kitchen and run around the table barking like a mad dog. When no one gets up to follow me, I close my jaws on Luke's pajama pants and try to drag him out of the kitchen forcibly.

"Hey, pal." He pats my head. "I know we're running late, but be patient, we'll go on your walk as soon as breakfast is over."

I don't care about my walk. Priscilla is sick.

I get up on my hind legs and howl.

Tegan is by my side immediately. "What's wrong, buddy?"

I bite her sleeve and drag her toward the door.

"I think he wants us to follow him."

Finally, someone who understands.

I bark another time impatiently, and then dash out. Tegan follows me into the living room and I bring her near the TV stand, whining with worry.

"Prissy," she says, and tries to touch the cat. "What's wrong with you?"

Priscilla claws at her and tries to snuggle further under, away from us and toward the wall.

"MOM!" Tegan shouts. "There's something wrong with Priscilla!"

In a heartbeat, all the humans are on their knees in front

of the TV, crowding the cat's space while she cowers away. They're making it worse; can't they see how scared she is?

I plant myself between them and the cat and growl at the humans to back off, showing some teeth for good measure.

"What is he doing?" Vivian asks, sitting back on her heels.

"I think he's protecting her?" Luke guesses.

"From us? I thought they hated each other?"

Luke stares at her with a cheeky grin. "Maybe at first, but the Hessington women have a way of growing on us."

"Gosh, you guys," Tegan chimes in. "Can you stop being cute for a second and see what's wrong with Priscilla?"

"Oh, I think I know," Luke says, and three heads—mine included—turn toward him.

"What?!" Tegan snaps, unable to bear the suspense. "Tell us."

"She's having kittens."

Kittens? We all turn our attention back to Priscilla.

"How can you tell?" Vivian asks.

Luke scratches the back of his head. "Well, there's a head coming out of her lady parts."

Tegan goes into problem-solving mode at once; she takes out her phone and does that thing humans call "googling" to get all the facts on helping a cat giving birth at home. She lists them aloud for everyone to hear.

Vivian sighs in disbelief. "Well, if someone had to run off and get pregnant, I'm glad it was the cat."

I squat down on the floor at a respectful distance and look at Priscilla to give her strength and encouragement.

Come on, kitty, you've got this.

***

Two hours later, we have three beautiful kittens. Priscilla and her little ones have been moved into one of the cardboard boxes Luke and I used to move our stuff into this house. And Vivian has stuffed the makeshift kennel with a layer of old newspapers and warm blankets before placing it near the radiator where they can keep the warmest. Luke lights the fireplace to make everything even cozier.

And I know that, technically, the kittens aren't mine—even if the little calico cutie looks a lot like me, she has all my colors, and we share the exact same orange eye patch—but I'm not the kind of dog who leaves a single mother to fend for herself. And if I ever come across the alley cat who did this to Priscilla, I'm going to chase him off the end of the Earth.

I peek my head above the lower wall of the box. All three kittens are snuggled close together at Pricilla's side, nursing. She's looking at her litter like a satisfied mama. When she spots me, her eyes swell even bigger with pride. I did this, she seems to want to tell me. I made these.

I move my head closer to hers until our noses almost touch and give her a small lick. She lets me. It's a start.

Yep, we're going to be a big, happy family.

The End

Hey, psst… In case you were wondering what happened to all those people Luke and Vivian went on dates with, here's how things turned out:

Meadow, the witch, was matched with Roger, and they fell head over heels in love at first sight. To this day, his mother is convinced he's been cursed. At least now, all three of them believe in magic.

Christopher decided he was too focused on his literary art to waste time on dates. He quit the agency and is still working on his unpublished masterpiece.

Sonia was picked up by a reality show called *Influence This,* where her quirk for confusing words made for some hilarious TV and skyrocketed her to the position of fans' number one favorite. Sonia also has developed a crush on that cute assistant director. He brings her coffee every morning, but still hasn't asked her out.

Carla finally found the courage to attend a Flat Earthers conference, where she met plenty of open-minded men. She started dating one of them and, together, they spend all their free time conducting experiments to prove the Earth is, indeed, flat. Their YouTube channel already has a hundred thousand views.

After her date with Luke, Mira felt a little wistful and decided to go to a bar alone where she met someone the old-fashioned way. They're still dating, and she's never been happier.

The End, for real this time…

Note from the Author

Dear Reader,

I hope you enjoyed *Opposites Attract*. If you'd like to spend more time in this world try the next book in the series, *I Have Never,* the story of Blair and her hot British boss.

Now I have to ask you a favor. If you loved my story, **please leave a review** on Amazon, Goodreads, your favorite retailer's website, or wherever you like to post reviews (your blog, your Facebook wall, your bedroom wall, in a text to your best friend...). Reviews are the best gift you can give to an author, and word of mouth is the most powerful means of book discovery. If you want to help me keep my work meaningful and for me to write more stories you'll love, leaving a review will go a long way.

I hope I haven't bored you too much with my babbling... Thank you for your constant support!

Camilla, x

Acknowledgments

Thanks to all of you for downloading this book. My readers are my strength and without your constant support, I wouldn't keep pushing through the blank pages.

Thank you to Rachel Gilbey for organizing the blog tour for this book and to all the book bloggers who participated. I love being part of your community.

Thank you to my street team, and to all of you who leave book reviews. They're so appreciated.

Thank you to my editors and proofreaders, Michelle Proulx, Helen Baggott, and Jennifer Harris, for making my writing the best it could be.

And lastly, thank you to my family and friends for your constant encouragement.

Cover Image Credit: Created by Freepik